Choose Me, Cowboy

Choose Me, Cowboy

A Canadays of Montana Romance

Barbara Ankrum

TULE
PUBLISHING

Dedication

To David, my love, for listening to every word. You helped me walk this book out daily with your encouragement and humor on our morning hikes. I couldn't do it without you. Mmwwwhaaa!

Chapter One

FOR A GIRL who wasn't born yesterday, Kate Canaday had the sneaking suspicion she'd been *had* by the two people in her life she cared most about. If they weren't all sitting in Grey's Saloon on a noisy Saturday night with a hundred people she knew, or at least recognized, as witnesses, she might have lost her temper.

Instead, she slid a disbelieving look between her sister, Eve, and her step-sister, Olivia, as the country music band cranked up behind them.

"So, let me get this straight," she said after taking a calming sip from her grapefruit vodka spritzer. "You two didn't just randomly join me here for a night out? Just because you've missed me and love me and thought a get-together would be fun? You came here for a…a *dating* intervention?"

Eve, the fairer of her two sisters, blinked and flicked a sideways plea for help to Olivia, who quickly said, "*Intervention?* Well, that's completely inaccurate."

"Totally. Inaccurate," Eve agreed, tucking a blond strand of misplaced hair behind her ear, looking lost.

Except that they'd spent the last five minutes breaking down Kate's questionable dating history and her habit of falling quickly—then dumping—every man she dated after a few short weeks. But mostly, their concern was about her current problem-in-residence, Cree Malone, the lead singer of the band playing on Grey's small stage right now.

Kate leaned toward them to be heard over the sound of the music, her long, auburn hair falling against her cheek. "What exactly would you call it, then? This little get-together?"

"Sisterly concern?" Olivia ventured with a sheepish look.

"Over my dating habits in general? Or about Cree?"

"His name isn't Cree, Kate. It's *Charlie*," Olivia corrected, "and he was in glee club with my best friend, Zena, in eleventh grade."

Kate narrowed a look at her. "I know his name. Of course, I know his name. He's in a band. It's his persona." The hairs on the back of her neck rose. "*Wait.* Did Dad and Jaycee put you up to this?"

"No!" they answered in unison, then exchanged guilty looks.

"They…might know we're doing this," Eve admitted in a small voice.

"*This*, meaning the *intervention*," Kate clarified.

"Stop calling it that." Olivia pulled her dark hair into a one-handed ponytail around her shoulder. "We just care about you and we're worried. Listen, it's no secret that you've had at least a dozen boyfriends this year—"

"That's a gross exaggeration," Kate said, tapping her nails on the table. "The figure's closer to ten."

"—and we haven't met a single one."

Kate sent them an incredulous look. "Why would you want to *meet* them? None of them was serious."

"Exactly!" Olivia slapped her beer bottle down on the table and the crown erupted in a little plume of foam. As she scrambled to mop up the mess with napkins, she said, "None of them was even your type."

"How do *you* know my type?"

"Were they?" Eve asked, her voice tinged with disbelief. She hooked a thumb in Cree's direction. "Is *he?*"

"My type?" Kate shook her head. "Yes." *No. Wasn't that the point?* The men she dated were like…like seat-fillers at awards ceremonies. One person vacates and another takes his place. Simple as that.

Behind them, her latest seat-filler, the *very* good-looking lead singer, '*Cree*', better known to mere mortals in nearby Livingston circles as Charlie Malone, had been belting out a drinking song about dirt roads, pick-up trucks and hot girls in cutoff shorts. No one would argue his talent. He'd probably be in Nashville within the year. With that rockabilly dark hair, those blue eyes and his penchant for ink, he looked like every other musician these days. He'd even inscribed her name on a small, blank spot on his forearm—a poor decision from which she'd tried to dissuade him. But her name was already lost there in his sleeve of tattoos and she supposed he could always turn the thing into a spiral or a cat or something that would blend in.

Before the next song, after he played an expert riff on his guitar, he pointed to Kate with a possessive nod, then punctuated that look with an onstage guzzle of beer. Several girls at the front tables who looked barely old enough to *be* in this bar, squealed for his attention.

Kate wondered where their parents were.

"This song's for my sexy, red-haired lady, Katie-Kat Canaday, sitting right over there," he purred a little drunkenly into the microphone. He followed this horrifying mangling of her name with an embarrassing cat yowl.

With all eyes suddenly on her, Kate slid down in her chair. Beside her, Eve and Olivia shared a private, confirming eye roll.

"What?" Kate said from behind the hand shielding her eyes. "It's not like I'm going to *marry* him. He's performing."

Olivia gestured with a meaningful tip of her head toward a nearby table, where the Bellmers—parents of one of her current kindergarten students—were staring at her with undisguised horror after Cree's shout out to her, their red wine glasses frozen halfway to their mouths.

Drat. She would hear about this one on Monday. And here it was, barely September and only two weeks into the school year. She pasted on her most professional smile and finger-waved at the Bellmers, who turned away whispering to one another.

"Look, I'm not one to judge, Kate," Olivia said, leaning across the table. "That's not what this is about. But your life is not exactly…you know, *uncomplicated*. You're a kindergarten teacher, in a very small town. And a guy like that? He will ruffle some feathers."

She knew that. Of course she did. Most of the men she'd dated were lower profile than Cree, and she had no rational answer as to why she'd agreed to go out with him.

"Technically speaking," she said in her own defense, and not a little bitterly, "I'm a laid-off kindergarten teacher. Long-term sub doesn't quite qualify." She'd been caught in a 'last-in, first-out' situation when budget cuts had forced layoffs. The school had kept her employed, temporarily, thanks to the beloved kindergarten teacher, Bette Moynihan, whose mother had the good grace to break her leg this month and suddenly needed Bette's help.

"You know they'll hire you back full time next year, as soon as the budget thingy gets resolved," Eve said. "They love you there."

Whether they did or not was a moot point. Their budget thingy was about to become her budget thingy. Bette was due back in November and she was counting the days and her pennies.

Still, she supposed she was simply pushing the envelope with Cree, but, truthfully, her life felt like it was starting to fly out of control like a spin painting, with bits of her casting about, looking for a handhold.

Reluctantly, she admitted that Olivia and Eve might have a small point, at least where Cree was concerned. She wasn't sure why she was defending him anyway. His boy-friend 'sell-by' date had expired two nights ago when—*and she shivered at the memory*—he'd drunkenly licked her cheek like a standard poodle in lieu of a kiss when he'd said goodnight. Which was the last in a short, but consistent list of line-crossings that had effectively ended them.

They were over. Cree just didn't know that yet.

Maybe ten boyfriends in one year *was* a bit indulgent. A*ll right*—excessive. But in her own defense, most of them had lasted less than three weeks and it wasn't as if she'd gone looking for love, or pined over each one she'd left. She wasn't interested in love. Or commitment. Or anything that could break her heart again. She just wanted to have fun. Was that so wrong?

"C'mon, Kate. You know you're better than him," Olivia said gently. "You deserve more than a wanna-be rock-star like 'Cree' Malone, that you picked up at the grocery store."

Kate flicked a finger around the rim of her glass with irri-tation. "First, I didn't pick him up. For the record, it was the other way around. And second," she said, pointing at the ceiling, "if you two have got *Yente* from 'Fiddler on the Roof' stashed somewhere around here to '*match me a match*' or '*catch me a catch*,' you can forget it. I don't do blind dates. I pick my own disasters, thank you very much."

Eve clucked and leaned in to Olivia with a dramatic sigh. "Darn. And we went to all that expense."

Kate fake smiled at them. "Maybe you two should just be happy for me that I'm not spending my evenings alone, turning into some spinster schoolteacher. I am perfectly capable of setting boundaries, knowing what's good for me and *what*, for heaven's sake, I *deserve*." She gulped a sip of vodka. "Besides, I can stop any time I want."

"*Hunh.* I dare you," Eve challenged flatly.

Kate gave a little snort. "What?"

"I dare you to stop dating. Take a break. Reconnoiter. Go cold turkey."

Cold turkey? Phhhhfft! Of course, she could. It wasn't like she had a *problem*. She could be alone. Entertain herself on a Friday night. Or…or a Saturday.

She *could*. She was almost sure she could.

Even as that thought formed, an adorable *maybe* twenty-one-year old drunk guy in a mechanic's shirt and a bottle of beer in his hand, sidled up to Eve. "Hey, darlin'," he yelled over the music, attempting to peer down the opening of her shirt. "D'you believe in love at first sight, or… should I walk by again?"

Eve sent Kate a slow burn and mouthed, "Watch and learn." She turned back to him, dragged a look up and down him, then said, "No. And *no*."

After a three-second beat, he said, "Well…a'right, then."

The mechanic chugged his beer and wandered off toward the front of the bar.

Turning back to Kate, Eve lifted her hands as if to say, *See? It's just that easy.*

Olivia bit her lip to keep from laughing.

Kate twisted her mouth to keep from doing the same. "Are you implying that if I wanted to, I couldn't—" she began, but she lost track of her thought as, across the bar, past the smoky haze, she caught sight of a cowboy whose back was to her. He seemed to be deep in conversation with someone in the shadows. Maybe her reaction was simply to his shirt, a familiar, fitted denim, hugging the contours of his strong back and arms. Or the way he stood, one knee cocked, like he used to just before a ride.

Maybe it was the vodka she was drinking.

But the Pavlovian tightening down low inside her, the slam of her heart against the cage of her ribs hit her as hard as always when she caught glimpses of men who looked like *him.* Men from the back. Men from the side. Men in shadows.

Like seeing a ghost.

Like all the times she'd thought she'd caught sight of her Grandma Chrissy after she'd passed, tottering down some street beside a stranger, or waving her frail arm outside a car window, or hearing her whisper in the middle of the night. And, for that split second, wishful thinking had her imagining the old woman could actually reappear.

But *he* wasn't a ghost and he wasn't dead—as far as she knew, though she'd made a point not to follow him or his career, not to be curious. No, he wasn't dead. Just dead to *her*. And that couldn't be him, anyway, she decided, studying the man across the bar. Because *he* was in Missoula or Denver or Albuquerque…riding on the back of some bull or making sweet forever with *what's-her-name* and their—

"—you couldn't…what? Kate?" Olivia was asking, but her gaze was searching out the corner that so fascinated Kate.

Dragging her eyes deliberately away from his doppelganger, Kate took another gulp of her drink. Maybe it was the sight of him that made her decide. Or maybe she was just tired of men of Cree's questionable ilk. Whatever the reason, she blurted, "Okay. Fine."

"*Fine?*" Eve jerked a confused look back at her. Olivia looked skeptical.

"You're on," she elaborated. "The dare. Just to prove you wrong."

A small victorious smile—or possibly relief—passed between her two sisters and Kate felt herself shrink a little.

Job done. Crisis averted. All was right with the world again.

"No dating for one month," Eve said, flattening her palm on the table.

Kate shrugged. "Done."

"Two?" Olivia suggested.

"Don't push your luck. If I win, it's hands off me and my dating life. If I lose…?"

9

"We have Yente on standby," Eve assured her.

"What about Cree?" Olivia glanced pointedly at the singer high-fiving the pretty girls near the stage.

Kate stared down at her empty drink. "Yeah, well… that *is* a shame. But some sacrifices just have to be made. I suppose I'll just have to break his heart."

And when she looked back, the ghost she'd glimpsed in the corner was gone.

IT WAS NEARLY ten when Finn Scott opened the door to his ranch house to the sound of the low hum of the television. The place was a mess of moving boxes, some he'd never even unpacked from the last move. Most of the lights were turned down and the rest of the house was blissfully quiet. As he came through the door, Izzy McCallum, who'd been horizontal on the couch watching a show, sat up.

"Oh. Hey," she said, yawning. She reached automatically for her hoodie, backpack and loose papers. Izzy, a blue-eyed twenty-year-old student, whose curly orange hair suited her quirky look, made a fruitless attempt to smooth down her wild mop. "How did everything go?"

He'd spent the evening haggling with Lodi Greenwall over the price of a bull. Not just any bull, either. The one that would be the foundation for his business.

"I think we reached an agreement," he told her with a tired smile. *Now it's just a matter of money.* "Thanks for watching the hooligans for me today. How were they?"

She got to her feet with a tired smile. "Honestly? They kinda missed you today."

He inhaled sharply and turned away to toss his keys onto the entryway table. Guilt stabbed at him, as happened most days lately when it came to the kids. Despite being the weekend, this whole day had been consumed with business.

"And Cutter," she went on, "decided tonight was the perfect time to practice his wall art—don't worry, I used a magic eraser on it—and Caylee was a perfect angel—complete with glitter glued to her '*wings.*' Of course, I took a picture." She quickly texted him the photo and his cell gave a little buzz. "But they were really good for me. I fed them dinner, gave them both baths and they've been down, without a peep, since seven-thirty."

He'd missed his small window of time with them tonight after the day he'd had, and he always regretted when that happened. Sometimes it felt like everyone was raising his children, but him.

He peeled off a few twenties and handed them to Izzy. He had her on a small salary, but today's overtime and this evening's meeting were extra. "You're a lifesaver. Thanks. You look as tired as I feel. Go home."

"About Monday," she said. "I have a bio-chem exam at two, so I can't pick them up after school, but I can meet you at the school playground and watch them while you have your parent-teacher conference at four-thirty. Does that work?"

It would have to. "Thanks, Izzy. We'll make it work."

She walked to the door and smiled back at him. "See you Monday, then."

"Night. Thanks again." He closed the door quietly behind her. For a moment, he just stood there, staring at the sparsely furnished room, still filled with unpacked moving boxes.

This place, his new home, looked like it had accidentally wandered out of the 1970s, and had never found its way back. Walls that weren't covered in aging wallpaper were paneled with pine. Every room boasted a different—worse than the one before—shade of shag carpeting and the kitchen appliances were a god awful shade of avocado green. The bathroom faucet in the kids' bath ran only on cold, and the barn roof leaked so badly the whole thing might actually be a tear down.

But none of those things mattered. This ranch belonged to him now, and a wave of pure gratefulness washed over him.

Only a month ago, the man who'd lived here for forty years, Frank Greevy—Finn's bull-riding coach of the last decade—had died after a long illness, leaving a hole in his world he wasn't sure he could ever fill. In a gesture that caught him completely by surprise, Frank had left this place to him, free and clear, in his will. Frank had never been married, never had children, but he had a special attachment to Finn's twins. He supposed that was why he'd done it. So they wouldn't be vagabonds anymore, chasing work and, lately, the occasional rodeo when money was tight. That Frank would leave him this place, this beautiful land, had been an unexpected gift he'd never be able to repay.

So, the place didn't look like home yet. In time, they would fill it up with their own memories and make it feel like home. But right now, the house felt lonely. Probably because of what had happened tonight, he felt the emptiness here more keenly.

Bone tired, with muscles aching from every fence he'd repaired and every new post hole he'd dug, he needed another drink. He pulled a beer from the fridge and cracked it open. Leaning against the green-tiled counter with one hip, he sipped it, trying to push away the memory of seeing Kate and the idiot band boy calling her out in front of the whole bar.

Katie-Kat Canaday. My sexy red-haired lady.

His chest gave a squeeze and he took a quick gulp of beer. Seeing her again tonight after all these years—even from across the room—had caught him off guard. More accurately, the sight of her rocked him. Momentarily stole the strength from his legs as he stood, talking bulls with Greenwall. He'd literally had to shove a hand against the wall and turn his back on her to keep his balance.

Of course, he'd remembered Kate was from Marietta when he'd moved here at the beginning of August. But he'd hardly expected she'd still live here. She'd always talked about wanting to live in a big city somewhere. New York or maybe San Francisco. They'd talked about doing that together, in fact. Once. He'd expected her to do just that. But here she was, still living in Marietta, Montana, about as far from a big city as a place could get. And, like an idiot, like an abandoned dog who couldn't let go, so was he.

The six years since their break-up in Missoula had done nothing to diminish the primal ache that always flashed over him like heat lightning at the sight of her. That shouldn't have surprised him. She'd appeared in his dreams with some regularity since that awful day and he'd wake hard and aching with want. That ache was in him now, even thinking about her.

Her hair was still that red color women were always trying to get out of a bottle, but never could. And she wore her hair long now, not short like when he'd known her. Perversely, all he could think as he'd watched her, was how that silky hair would feel, brushing against the skin of his bare chest.

He let out a humorless sound that echoed around the half-empty room. That said just about everything there was to say about how well he'd gotten over her.

She hated him for good reason. He owed it to her to stay far away. But he hadn't expected her to be tangled up with an idiot like the lead singer from that band. Maybe she'd changed since their time together. Maybe that tattooed freak was her type now.

Six years and the whole world had turned inside out. For damned sure, his world had. His life had spun like an off-balance top for a while after the divorce. But here, he sensed, things were different. Now that he'd settled in Paradise Valley—a place that took his breath away and had already settled into his bones like he belonged there—he'd decided that he'd found where he wanted to be.

A sharp knock at the door made him jump.

Izzy, he thought automatically, scanning the coffee table for whatever she'd forgotten. But he could see nothing. He went to the door and pulled it open. "What did you forget?" he was asking before he saw not Izzy, but a man in a black cap and 80's style Members Only jacket standing at his doorstep.

"Can I help you?" he asked.

"Finn Scott?"

"Yeah?" A bad feeling crawled up the back of his neck and he had the impulse to slam the door in the stranger's face. "What do you want?"

"Just this." The man pulled an envelope out of a breast pocket and shoved the thing into Finn's hands. "You've been served."

He stared down at the envelope uncomprehendingly at first as the man took his leave and headed down the walkway. His insides gave a twist and he scowled after him, realizing he must have been lurking outside, waiting for him to come home so he could slap these papers in his hand.

He wanted to shout after him, tell him specifically where he could stick them. Because he already knew what they were. Though he wouldn't have admitted this to anyone—that would have meant he thought of her at all—he'd been half-waiting for her to pull something since day one. He closed the door, with no gentleness, ripped open the envelope and scanned the court papers. *"Motion To Modify Court Ordered Custody of Minor Children..."*—Damn her!—*"Plaintiff, Melissa Jamison."*

Jamison. Not Scott. So, sometime in the past four years, she'd managed to drag another sucker into her path of destruction. He actually felt sorry for him. For a moment.

As he read on, he found the kicker buried in the middle of a paragraph, three pages in. *"Plaintiff intends to move to Hong Kong with her husband and seeks permission to take the children out of the country in the within custody modification."*

He braced a hand on the wall behind him with a foul curse. *Hong Kong?*

From around the corner, five-year-old Cutter, one-half of the dynamic-duo that owned him, body and soul, came stumbling toward him, rubbing his eyes. Without a word, Finn set the papers down, scooped the boy into his arms and hugged him fiercely to him. "Hey, Snip," he murmured. The boy's white-blond hair smelled of shampoo and sleep and Cutter's own sweet fragrance. "What are you doing up?"

"Daddy," Cutter said tearily against his neck. "I had a bad dream."

He sifted his fingers through the boy's sweaty hair. "You're okay now. I'm here." He started back with Cutter toward the boy's room.

"There was a monster in my room," Cutter murmured.

He nodded. "We'll just see about that. No monsters allowed. That's the rule, right?"

Cutter nodded fiercely and sniffled. He settled the child into his bed beside the one where Caylee slept, then knelt down beside him. "Here we go." He checked under the bed, behind the curtains and crawled to the small closet and opened it. "All clear." Then he reached for the jar of glitter Cutter's twin kept on the nightstand between them for occasions such as this. He unscrewed the top and tossed a pinch of glitter into the air, thankful none of the hard-bitten cowboys he spent his days with could see him now. He'd never hear the end of that. "No self-respecting monster would dare come in here now."

The glitter had been Caylee's idea and seemed to satisfy Cutter's feeling that magic was afoot and dragons had been slayed. He found himself wishing that glitter would work just as easily on those papers in the living room.

He kissed the boy, who was a miniature version of him, and rubbed his back until his small chest rose and fell with deep regular breaths. When he was sure that neither of them would stir, he went back to the living room and punched in a number on his cell. The hour was late and his old college roommate, now an attorney, Mark Erlewine, in Missoula, answered the phone, sounding groggy.

"This better be good, buddy," Mark growled on the other end. "I have court in the morning."

"She did it, Mark," he said without preamble. "She served me with papers tonight. She's trying to get them back."

A deep sigh on the other end. "Read me the caption and the first two pages of the complaint."

He did and when he'd finished, Erlewine asked, "When's the court date again?"

"At the end of the month. In Missoula."

"The judge? His name should be listed on the stamp."

He scanned down the document. "Corillo."

On the other end of the line, his attorney made a strangled sound and fell silent, thinking.

"When you get quiet, I know I'm in trouble," Finn said. "I *am* in trouble, aren't I?"

"Corillo is ultraconservative. Big on family stability. And he favors mothers. I'm sorry to hear she's filed a motion to reconsider, but I can't say I'm actually surprised. This kind of thing happens all the time. Situations change. People change their minds. And if, by trouble, you mean are you at risk of losing full custody? Well, yes. She's their mother. If she'd signed over all rights to them when she gave you full custody three and a half years ago, this would be a different story. We can argue abandonment, but it's a risk. A big one, considering your situation."

"My situation?"

"Look, I know what kind of father you are, but your life, from the outside, has a tangle of loose ends. You need to show stability. Roots, even."

"I just signed the final papers on a small ranch I was lucky enough to inherit here in Marietta. I'm only doing the rodeo thing temporarily to earn enough money to get that going."

"The ranch is good. But one card trumps the rest. If you were married...stable, things might look different to a judge like Corillo."

"*Married?* He can't discriminate against me for being single. Can he?"

"No. Not technically. But that doesn't mean he can't rule against you. We could file for dismissal at this hearing and might get it. But we might not. My best advice? Find a wife, Finn. And find one fast. Get yourself looking settled. If you don't, your crazy ex may just get what she wants."

KATE SWIPED THE chalk-clogged eraser over the board at the back of her classroom at Marietta Elementary. At the end of a very long Monday full of kindergarteners, an awkward conversation with Judy Elsworth, the principal, regarding a phone call she'd gotten from the Bellmers about Saturday night, and a handful of parent-teacher conferences, she longed for nothing more than a glass of wine, a plate of homemade pasta and a foot massage, not necessarily in that order. But since her term of forced solitude was upon her, the foot massage was, unfortunately, not in the cards. Wine and pasta, alone, would have to suffice.

With a sigh, she glanced at her watch as she gathered up her things. Nearly five-thirty. Her last scheduled parent/teacher conference had cancelled at the last minute and rescheduled for tomorrow. Which meant another long day. But she actually didn't mind conference time. She looked forward to getting to know the families of the children in her class, even if the class was only hers temporarily. She already knew many of them. In a town the size of Marietta, practically everyone knew everyone, for better or for worse.

Glancing out the window, she noticed thunderheads gathering in the sky. Something was coming. Weather tended to move fast over the mountains, coming and going with a speed that matched the dramatic Montana landscape. She'd better get a move on, she thought, before getting caught in a thundershower.

On the near-empty playground, she noticed two of her favorites, Caylee and Cutter, five-year-old twins from Janice Brinker's kindergarten class, climbing the taller of two geodesic dome jungle gyms on the now-empty playground. She guessed that Janice had a parent-teacher conference scheduled for today, too. The twins were the exception to the *everyone-knew-everyone* rule. As they were new to town, no one knew much about them at all, except that they'd just moved to Marietta before the start of school in mid-August.

On a nearby bench, head bent to her cell phone, was the young woman Kate had often seen picking up the pair at school. She was not their mother, Kate had been told, but a babysitter.

As Kate watched, Cutter—with typical five-year-old audacity—stood straight up on the climbing structure and twirled his arms like a bird. Kate gasped and pressed a helpless palm to the window. "Look up. *Look up!*" she begged the woman through the thick glass.

And just as the woman did look up, Caylee's high-pitched squeal accompanied her brother's pinwheel off the monkey bars toward the rubber mats below.

With a gasp, Kate dropped everything in her arms and ran. Slamming through the push-bar doorway at the end of the hall, she raced outside feeling like everything was happening in slow motion. The slow whoosh of blood in her ears, the sound of her shoes against the asphalt as she ran toward the playground and the boy lying at the base of the jungle gym.

The babysitter was holding the crying boy by the time she reached the monkey bars and Kate reached up to pull Caylee down safely. But the little girl hung back under the bars, staring wide-eyed at her brother. For his part, Cutter had relinquished every bit of his five-year-old bluster and was wailing loudly.

"I-It's all my fault," a distraught babysitter told Kate as

she dropped down beside them. "I took my eyes off him for a moment and—"

"Is his head okay?"

Izzy had a hand clapped over her mouth. "I think so. It's his arm. He landed badly. It might be broken."

There was no question in Kate's mind that was indeed the case. His wrist was already turning black and blue and beginning to swell.

From behind her came the sound of someone running and she looked up as a man dropped to his knees beside the boy. He scooped the boy away from the young woman and into his own arms and sat on the rubber mat, his back half-turned to Kate. "Hey, Snip, it's okay, now. I'm here. Oh, man. That looks like it hurts." He half-turned to the young woman. "I *pay* you to watch them, Izzy," he said sharply. "What the hell happened?"

The sound of his voice made her breath hitch. Kate watched the man sooth a hand over the boy's forehead and kiss him there and she felt her world tilt sideways.

Oh, no. It couldn't be.

No, really, it couldn't. But he turned to look at Izzy and all doubt vanished.

Finn Scott. Her *Finn Scott.* Scratch that. There weren't enough possessive pronouns in the world to make him hers.

"It's my fault," Izzy was saying. "The twins were playing tag and I looked away for a moment and Cutter was—I'm so sorry."

Twins? He and what's-her-face had had twins?

"It was a accident, Daddy," Caylee said. "Cutter was being a bird."

Inconsolable, the boy buried his face against his father's broad chest. Behind him, thunder rumbled across the prairie and a streak of lightning jagged across the sky. The heat from that jagged flash seemed to explode in her chest as he looked up, noticing her for the first time.

The instinct to run rolled through her like the thunder that rumbled across the sky and she scooted back away from him, hoping that he'd forgotten her as she'd tried to forget him. But she wasn't that lucky.

Recognition, mixed with confusion, burned in his dark gaze. "*Kate?*"

He turned fully then, looking at her starkly with those brown-green-gold eyes. Eyes that had once had the power to melt her into a puddle of want and need. Those eyes brought to mind long, athletic Saturday mornings, sharing a thoroughly rumpled bed and slow, deep kisses.

Doomed. I am doomed.

A numb buzzing started up in her ears that had nothing at all to do with the nearby thunder.

She couldn't think straight. Finn was sitting two feet away from her, holding his son and she couldn't imagine what she should be doing with her hands.

And then she remembered Saturday night. No doppelganger. No ghost. It was him. Right here in Marietta. The *hell?*

"That's Miss Candy," Caylee said, using the name most of the five-year-olds used for her. "She's not our teacher. She's the other one."

"That's me," she admitted in a small voice. "The other one.*"*

Her words elicited the proper response, a wince from Caylee's father.

"Scott's a pretty common last name around here," she managed. "I never—I didn't connect them with you."

He rubbed a hand across his mouth and said, *"You're* Miss Candy?"

Izzy, who'd been wallowing in self-reproach, now flicked a curious look at them over the steeple of her fingers, apparently relieved no one was looking at her anymore.

"I am," Kate said, getting to her feet, "but I suppose if you'd ever come to school with your kids, you would have known that." She instantly regretted the sharp bite of those words, but there was no taking them back now. Belatedly, she remembered what little she knew about him and the words 'single-dad' came to mind. Which meant…. A whole jumble of chaos kicked off in her brain.

Finn used to get a look on his face just before he nodded to the gate-puller, when he was all tucked and tied onto the back of some bred-to-be-vicious bucking-bull, his hand clamped down hard by the leather strap, his hat pushed down low over his eyes. He wore a look that said, 'I'm ready,' or 'I'm all in.' or 'Don't mess with me.' He looked at her that way now as he got to his feet with his little boy in his arms.

She was a terrible person.

"I've got to get him to an ER," Finn said. "Can you point me towards one?"

"Is my arm b-broke, Daddy?" Cutter whimpered.

"We'll see," he answered, kissing the boy's forehead again. "I hope not, Snip."

"The Marietta Regional Hospital is just down at the other end of town," Kate told him. "Across from the fairgrounds on Railroad Ave."

He turned around in a circle with the boy in his arms. "Railroad Ave….?"

"If you turn right out of the—it's just down this way a bit and then…oh, never mind. I'll take you." Seriously, she thought a little wildly, she should have her head examined for blurting that out without a thought to the consequences. "Or," she amended, "maybe it's better if Izzy takes you?"

Izzy sniffed and brushed her wet cheeks with the base of her palms. "Or I could take Caylee home with me until you're finished at the ER," she offered. "I promise, Mr. Scott, she'll be fine. If Miss Candy drives you, that is."

"Canaday," Kate corrected, shifting uneasily and looking at the sky. Rain was starting to fall. Small droplets splattered on the playground nearby.

"Oh. I'm sorry," Izzy said. "I've only heard about you as

Miss Candy."

She shook her head. "They all call me that. And it's probably better if Caylee doesn't have to sit in the ER waiting. She must be hungry."

"You sure?" he asked Kate.

Not at all. "Yes," she said. "I'll just get my keys and purse from my classroom. I know an Orthopedic doc at the hospital. Ben Tyler. I'll give him a call on the way."

He gave her a tight nod, then turned to his daughter. "Caylee, you'll be okay with Izzy for a few hours?"

"We'll have dinner and make cookies, Caylee. Just you and me," Izzy assured her, but Caylee clung to her father.

She was taller than average, as Cutter was. Long, yet petite, with delicate, pretty features that had his DNA written all over them. Kate's heart squeezed a little. How she could have missed that in the last two weeks on the playground, when these two children were just children and didn't yet belong to Finn? To him and to the woman Kate had—over the years—come to think of as *She Who Shall Not Be Named.*

"But what about Cutter?" Caylee asked, eyes watering. "He might need me."

"I'll take good care of him." Finn bent low and kissed the top of her head. "He'll need you to sign his cast when he gets home. You'll be first in line."

Kate blinked and stared down at her shoes. She would not be swayed by his tenderness with his children. Nor would she revise her feelings for the twins who—through no fault of their own—had once acted as both fulcrum and lever to pry away the life she'd hoped for. They were blameless. The same could never be said of their father.

"It'll be okay, Cutter. Bye, Miss Candy." Caylee had her father's big, hazel eyes and she turned them, to full effect, on Kate now.

She tucked a strand of Caylee's blonde hair behind her ear and felt something in her chest twist. She was a child who often seemed particularly in need of hugs from the female teachers in school. Could she have been drawn to her all along by the invisible thread that connected them all? "Bye, Caylee," she whispered. "See you tomorrow on the playground?"

Caylee nodded and started toward the parking lot with Izzy.

Without further adieu, Kate back-peddled toward her classroom and called back to the man she'd left behind, "I'll be right back."

He just stood there, watching her go, his eyes locked on hers. So, she did the only thing a good self-preservationist would do. She turned and ran.

Chapter Two

SEVEN-THIRTY CAME AND went and Kate's stomach growled as she paced the small, curtained-off ER room across the bed from Finn. Ben Tyler, the handsome orthopedic surgeon she'd met through Olivia's boyfriend, Jake Lassen, had luckily been on shift tonight and had set Cutter's arm. He was smoothing the last of the plaster tape, whose fragrance mingled damply with the sterile hospital smell. His cast was, by Cutter's own choosing, a bright, neon green and would soon be decorated with copious stickers and well wishes at school.

"Luckily," Ben told Cutter, "you got the last of the cool, green color. Everyone else who breaks an arm tonight will have to settle for a boring white or...pink."

Cutter shuddered at that prospect. "I do not like pink."

"Understood." He pulled off his gloves, took something out of his pocket and handed it to the boy. Cutter opened his fist to reveal a colorful rubber tree frog. "I only give these to kids who are especially brave. Think you can handle him?"

A smile creased Cutter's mouth. The first of the evening.

He nodded and jumped the frog across his chest.

"So," Finn said quietly to Ben, "no problems later on with the bone?"

Washing the plaster off his hands, Ben said, "Growth-wise? No. No growth plate involved, or I would have called a pediatric ortho down from Livingston for a consult. This is a clean, non-displaced fracture. It'll heal up in no time, and he'll be climbing play structures again and causing headaches for Dad. Right, Cutter?"

Cutter nodded sleepily. His bedtime had passed an hour ago, and the pain meds they'd given him had kicked in. Outside, they could hear the rain still pounding on the roof. Torrents slanted against the windows in a deluge Kate had hoped would abate before they had to go. Not likely.

"Thank you, Doc," Finn told Ben, his voice thick.

Ben nodded to them both. "Glad I was able to help. So, we're done here. I'll make sure they have your paperwork ready so you can go home." Ben gave Kate a kiss on the cheek and shook Finn's hand. "But I'd feed her, if I were you. She gets very cranky without meals."

Annoyed, she sat back down in an attempt to stop fidgeting, but gave Ben the stink eye. "Thank you for your oh-so professional opinion, Doctor Ben, but I am perfectly capable of feeding myself."

He turned a look back at her and winked.

She grinned, absently wondering why a doctor as cute as Ben was still single. And why, for that matter, *she'd* never dated him? All blond and beachy-looking, with brains as a bonus?

Not a place filler, she reminded herself. Dr. Ben Tyler would make someone a very nice husband someday, if he ever got his nose out of his medical journals. For being the cutest doctor in town, he was certainly the one with the fewest social skills. With the exception of that wink, of course.

When she looked back, she found Finn watching her, all dark and broody. She felt herself blush and looked away quickly. *Gads.* Was there anything more awkward than old lovers meeting this way?

"I'll be back when you're all set to go," Ben told them. "If I can speed up the process, I will. That shouldn't take long. It's still pouring out there."

Finn sighed and brushed a hand through Cutter's hair. "Close your eyes, Snip. It's okay if you fall asleep."

Cutter didn't have to be asked twice. Within moments, he and the frog were down for the count.

Across the ER cot, Finn's eyes met Kate's. There were a thousand questions between them that, quite possibly, neither of them wanted answered. Speaking strictly for herself, she just wanted to get out of this evening with her dignity intact. But probably too late for that, as well. She felt exhausted from the tension of the last two hours. Now, with no doctors, nurses or five-year-olds to interfere, they stared at each other across the entrenched battlements they'd spent years erecting between them.

"Thanks, Kate," he murmured, his gaze scanning her face. "For bringing us and hanging around. This isn't the first trip to the ER for him, but it's his first broken bone." The very word 'broken' had made him go pale and the worry lines around his eyes deepen.

"Like father like son, I suppose."

"I guess so."

She nodded. From what she'd witnessed tonight, he was all in as a father now. "*Twins*? Really, Finn? Two?"

"Oh, yeah." He gave a magnanimous shrug. "When I screw up, I do so in multiples. Not that I'd—" His gaze flicked up to her and color rose in those tanned cheeks of his.

"Not that you'd change a thing?" Kate finished. "Is that what you were going to say?"

Tight-lipped, he took the frog from Cutter's lax hand and stuffed the thing in his own pocket. "Yeah. I guess I was."

Her stomach cramped. "Well, I guess things all worked out for you then. You and—" she hesitated—"what's-her-face."

"I wouldn't change anything, except hurting you. But how could I regret them?" he asked, tucking Cutter's meaty, but small hand in his big one. "They're the good that came out of the bad."

Kate stood and turned her back to him so she could take a couple of deep breaths. "They *are* good. Both of them.

Even if they *are* yours," she added, just *because*. "Which, I had no idea about until tonight. What are you doing here? In Marietta, I mean. You must have remembered that this was where I'm from. Why would you—?"

"You really want to know?"

She wanted to know everything about him. Every last detail about his life since she'd seen him last. But her eagerness to answer all the questions that had nagged her for years would only make her look desperate. So she shrugged and stared past the curtain into the treatment room. "Never mind. I'm not really interested."

You didn't come for me. That's all I need to know.

Kate blinked. *Oh, dear God. Did I say that out loud?*

She turned back to him, relieved to find him staring at the bed. "Not that I care, but...what happened to the rodeo?"

"I walked away from it. Mostly. But that's a long story," he said.

He'd been a star, or at least a rising star on the rodeo circuit when he'd been hers. He should have been wildly successful by now, not drifting through Marietta on his way to somewhere else.

"Does the story involve a certain buckle bunny we both know?"

He sighed. "You wanna... come back to my place for some dinner?"

"No?" The word came out sounding ridiculously like a

question. She lifted her chin, and squinted back at him, just to eliminate any ambiguity. "I mean, *no*."

He shrugged. "You gotta eat."

"I don't have to eat with *you*."

"I'll cook."

She burned a look at him. "*You? Cook?*"

He smiled that old smile at her that always made her brain buzz. There was no justice in a universe where the man who had broken her heart into a million pieces, the man she'd spent the last six years hating, had only gotten more handsome with age. Not less. And he could still wield that smile that made her all her female parts go awry.

Curse him.

Nor had he lost any hair. His was still a thick, luxuriant mink brown, a little too long, but without a trace of grey or thinning as so many other guys their age had. Whatever he'd been up to the last six years, he appeared to only have gotten stronger. Her gaze strayed to his forearms, beneath his rolled up shirt sleeves and she remembered how, sometimes, just the sight of them used to make her want to jump him.

But those days were far behind them.

"I cook," he said, in answer to her question. "I do laundry. I do a lot of things that might surprise you."

"Oh, I think you're good in the surprise department." She'd meant that comment as a jab and she wasn't about to pull her punches with him. But for a man whose world had once revolved around defeating the meanest bulls alive, almost everything about him surprised her tonight. Not that that softened or did anything to change her feelings about him. He still did, and always would, occupy that same black hole in her life he had for the past six years.

But the devil in her wanted to ask him about his wife. And why he was a single dad? Was she, God forbid, somewhere here in Marietta, too? Did he still love her?

Common sense prevailed. In a few minutes, they'd be out of here. She'd drive him back to his car; she'd go her way and he'd go his. They'd keep to their separate corners in Marietta until he moved on. And that would be that.

But even as that decision finalized in her mind, he got slowly to his feet, rounded the bed and came over to stand beside her. Kate's eyes widened and she felt herself backing up against the sink. There was something in the way he moved, some deep sensuality or sense of purpose about him that always disarmed her. Maybe in the way he watched her through that dark sweep of lashes as he moved her way, like a big cat stalking its prey. But he held his palms up, indicating he meant no harm, and he stopped only a few feet away from her.

"What are you doing?" she asked in a hushed voice. "Go back to your side of the bed."

"Relax. I don't want to wake him." He leaned a hip against the counter, and folded his arms. "I'm not going to bite you."

"Maybe I should go and get the car—"

"I'm divorced, Kate," he said, almost as if he'd read her thoughts of a moment ago. "For the past four years."

Four years? Disappointment or anger or some other unrecognizable emotion sliced through her, sharp and quick. She did the mental math. That meant since the twins were under two? And never once had he come looking for her? Not, she corrected, that she'd wanted him to, aside from the overwhelming urge to punch him. But with her back up against the sink, she didn't want to indulge her curiosity about why he hadn't ever tried to find her. "I don't care," she told him, flatly.

She could tell he didn't believe her. When he twisted his mouth that way, that was a sure sign he was plotting something. "What about you?" he asked.

"What about me?"

"You never married?"

She shot a glance at her bare left hand where his gaze had landed, then curled her fingers into a fist, furious that he'd goaded her into looking. "No. Not," she added quickly, "because there haven't been…I just haven't—oh, it's none of your business, Finn. Seriously."

"I saw you the other night at Grey's."

Surprise thrummed through her for the hundredth time tonight. Had he been watching her while she'd been watching him? "Yeah? Well, I saw you, too. Although I wasn't sure that was you. In fact, I was certain it wasn't. Because I couldn't imagine what you'd be doing in *my home town.*"

"What happened to your dreams of going to the big city, Kate? New York? San Francisco?"

She hated him for remembering that. "They were just dreams. And dreams change. I'm a teacher. And I teach here. Well, part time now, anyway. And I love my job. My family is here. My life is here."

"I can see why you love it. It's a beautiful place, Marietta." As if to dispute that, the rain slashed against the window with a ferocious swipe that rattled the glass. She gave him nothing but her most ironic smile.

He changed tactics. "That singer, the other night, the one who called you out…?"

An involuntary shudder of memory tore through her. Of course, he'd heard him call her out. Of course, she could keep no illusion of dignity here, with her butt backed up to the sink. "Cree? What about him?"

"Are you…involved with him?"

"What could that possibly matter to you?"

He shrugged. "Are you?"

"No! He was just being…drunk." She peered through the curtain and down the corridor, hoping someone would be coming with their paperwork. No rescue was in sight. "I'm not dating anyone. I'm on a dating hiatus." *Drat!* Why had she told him that?

"Good. Then you can have dinner with me tonight." That smile again.

"I told you, I'm not dating anyone. *Especially* you."

"That's good, then. Because it won't be a date. It's a thank-you for helping us tonight. That's all. Will you let me cook you dinner?"

"No."

He tilted his head patiently. "It's been nearly six years—"

"Whose fault is that?"

Surprise caused a little tick between his brows. "I...I didn't think you'd want anything to do with me."

"You would have been right."

Liar.

Kate mentally slapped her inner critic and told her to shut up, despite, or maybe *because of* the flicker of hurt she saw in his eyes. All these years, she'd purposefully avoided any mention of him, refused to search him out on social media, or the regular media, afraid she'd see photos of his happy little family together where she should have been. Not that she cared anymore. She'd been over him for years. Forever.

She reminded herself of this, despite the fact that his standing so close to her, smelling as good as he did, made her want to touch him. Reach out and run her fingers along the hollows of his shadowed cheek and thread her fingers into his hair until he pulled her into his arms one last time.

Feeling dizzy at the thought, she knew a scenario like that one was not what she wanted. She was a reasonable person with a hair-trigger sense of self-preservation. And touching him—even in her imagination—would only set off a fire storm of trouble she did not want.

No. Finn showing up tonight was merely an annoyance and the sooner she moved past this and put him behind her, the better off she'd be. They could act like adults. Tie up this loose thread between them and put their history to rest. Maybe that was for the best. Maybe she'd been waiting to do this since the day he'd left her.

She exhaled sharply. "Fine. All right. I'll come. But it's just dinner. Nothing more. Understood?"

A nurse chose that moment to open the curtain with paperwork in her hand. She froze uncertainly, hearing the tense exchange. "Am I...interrupting?"

He took the papers and smiled at Kate. "No. You're just in time."

AFTER GETTING THE kids settled for the night, Finn put on some low music, poured Kate a glass of red wine and handed it to her in his avocado-colored kitchen. She took the glass reluctantly, arguing that she had school tomorrow, then gulped half of the wine down. He watched her with amusement over the rim of his own glass, understanding the impulse whole-heartedly.

He could see that she'd been surprised to follow him to the doorstep of this ranch. Everyone in town had known Frank Greevy and knew this place had been his forever. And very few knew about him or the will. If he wasn't mistaken, she was bursting with questions about what he was doing here, but she didn't ask one.

In the soft lighting, out of the daylight, her hair looked less red and more the deep burgundy color of that wine in her glass. He remembered how her hair used to change color that way, and how her eyes changed, chameleon-like, according to what she was wearing. The sea-green top she had on tonight turned them a grey-green color, but sometimes, they were the color of emeralds.

She'd grown into her beauty, and she was still long and lean. Athletic. Memories stirred of those long limbs of hers wrapped around him. Of long, slow kisses on summer nights like this one and sex that had left them exhausted, but happy. As good as that part of their lives had been—better than good—that was only part of what he missed about her the most. The other was simply this. Standing in their kitchen, sharing the day. Letting his gaze slide over her and imagining a future together.

Maybe spending his time around nothing but laconic cowboys and chatty five-year-olds had simply made him miss a grown woman's company. *This* grown woman's company.

As Van Morrison sang in the background about Tupelo Honey, Kate took another gulp, clutching her wine glass as if the thing were a floating seat cushion and she'd just found herself in the water.

"Better?" he asked, as he got the steaks into the pan.

She lingered at the fringes of his kitchen, checking out

his house as he worked on dinner. "Should I lie and say that glass of wine wasn't necessary? Or should I just admit that I might not get through this without this?"

"You could lie, but that first gulp was a dead giveaway," he said. "Besides, the truth is always better."

"Said the spider to the fly."

God, he'd missed her. He took a sip of his own wine, letting the alcohol soothe the tension from his throat. "So, I'm the spider?"

She smiled tightly. "That's not how I remember things, exactly, but there was some venom involved. Speaking of venom, where is she anyway? Your ex?"

"No clue," he answered, tossing some asparagus onto a broiler pan and dousing the veggies with a dash of salt, pepper and olive oil. "I haven't seen Melissa for years."

Surprise parted Kate's lips and she lowered her drink. "What? But...what about the kids?"

He shoved the pan under the broiler. "Turned out she liked the *idea* of being a mother better than actually *being* a mother."

Kate fluttered a look at the floor. "Oh. Finn..."

"Go on. You can say you told me so." God knew, he would if he were her.

"That would be spiteful," she said, running her finger along the rim of her glass. "And wrong. But you don't mind if I think that, do you?"

"No. I don't mind."

She wandered along his counter, touching the handful of spice jars lined up on a little rack, the toaster, a basket full of organic apples. "So…this…is all you. You and the twins."

He ripped up a handful of lettuce leaves and added them to a salad bowl. "There's Izzy. She's been essential, notwithstanding what happened tonight. I was lucky to find her when I got here. What about about you?" he asked, redirecting. "Have you been here since graduating?"

"Yes." She pulled open his refrigerator and looked inside. "I came home after I did my teaching practicum in Missoula and got a job. Here I am. I worked at the school for two years, then this summer I got laid off because of budget cuts. With the least amount of time there, I was the first to go. Right now, I'm a long-term sub, until the regular teacher comes back."

"How come you never married?" he said.

She took a gulp of wine. "I'm not in the market. Doesn't mean I don't date. Just," she added with the lift of one brow, "no one my family approves of. They seem to have…*opinions*."

"Then they must definitely hate me."

She shut the fridge door deliberately. "They never really knew about what happened with us. No one did."

He frowned, truly taken aback for the first time. A stab of something like hurt washed through him. But he supposed he didn't have the right to feel hurt about anything she did. "You never told your family about me? Even before…?"

She blushed and leaned her back against the fridge. "My family would have been all over us if they'd known I was dating you. They're like that. Not in a bad way, but call me superstitious. I didn't want to jinx it. Then…Italy. After we got engaged, I'd planned on taking you home that next weekend, and then, well, I guess we both know what happened to that plan."

After they'd broken up, she'd kept her hurt all to herself? But she was close to her family. That didn't make any sense to him. For the first time, he wondered if there had been more to their breakup than what he'd thought. Had she kept their relationship from her family because she wasn't sure they'd accept him? Or because she wasn't sure *she* did?

Cowboy. Bull rider. He came from a different world and his family was nothing like hers—rich, successful. He still had half a family. Just his mom. She lived in Florida now, far from the brutal Montana winters and he only saw her a few times a year. His father had been out of the picture since he was a boy.

Still, as he contemplated their ending—his and Kate's— he found himself wanting to explain himself again, revise, rewrite their ending, but, of course, it was too damn late for that. Moving forward. That had always been his only choice.

Dinner came together then and he turned to plate the food up. Kate found the silverware and set two place settings for them on the small dining room table. She refilled the wine glasses and they sat down to eat. She'd put the table between them and sat on the opposite side.

"Mmmm," she murmured after tasting the steak. "I must confess. This is really good."

"High praise."

"I'll give the Devil his due."

Her smile made his gut twist with a hunger that had nothing to do with steak.

"Though I must admit," she went on, "whenever I imagined you over the years, you as Mr. Mom never occurred to me."

"You *imagined* me?" he asked hopefully, returning her grin.

Color rose in her cheeks and her eye twitched. "Once or twice. But don't flatter yourself. I moved on long ago."

With guys like Cree, he thought. Tattooed musicians didn't fit his mental picture of the Kate he remembered. His Kate. But the universe had taken a substantial shift since they'd seen each other last. Anything could have happened, and probably had.

"So," she asked, without looking at him, "this used to be Frank Greevy's place, didn't it? Are you…renting until you move on?" She took another gulp of wine.

"I own this place now. Frank Greevy left the ranch to me when he passed."

She choked on her wine. When she finally stopped coughing, she managed to say, "You're *staying* in Marietta?"

Watching her with concern, he picked up his wine and

let the glass hover near his mouth for a moment before taking a sip. "I like it here. The kids like it. And apparently, they don't let you pick up five hundred acres and leave the county with them. So…yeah. I'm staying."

For a long beat, she just stared at him as if he'd just told her Darth Vader was her father. "I see."

"Don't take it too hard. Marietta's a small town, Kate, but it's not that small. If you don't want to see me I can make that happen." *But not if I can help it.*

"No, it's smaller than you think. Today's the perfect example."

He lifted his glass to her. "Speaking of which, I don't think I've properly thanked you for your help tonight." He touched her glass with a clink. "Thank you. What you did was real kind, considering."

She tilted her head and took a sip. "Cutter's a sweet boy. You've done well with him. With both of them."

He glanced behind him. "Whoa, I could've sworn that was a compliment that just shot past me."

"It was. Okay? Which does nothing to ameliorate my feelings about you being *here*."

"*Am-eliorate?*" He rubbed his jaw. "*Huh.* I might have to look that one up."

She rolled her eyes. "Alter. Change. *Improve.*"

A grin crept to his mouth. He'd forgotten how much fun it was to tease her. "Uh-huh. I get you. Well, I know this place doesn't look like much now, but I'm gonna *ameliorate* it. The house has good bones and a lot of potential, don't you think?"

She cast a furtive look around his personal time warp. "I wasn't referring to the house."

He leaned back in his chair and toyed with his glass, enjoying the way the light from the 70's chandelier cast her skin in porcelain light. "Right."

"Exactly what do you plan to do with this five-hundred-acre gift?" she asked, forking in a mouthful of salad.

"Run some cattle. Start a bucking bull breeding business."

Those green eyes flicked up to his. "That sounds expensive."

Money was the last thing he intended to discuss with her, especially when there were so many other topics that came to mind. Like when he was going to see her again. Or if she ever intended to forgive him. His gaze drifted to her hair and his fingers itched to touch it. "I'm good. Hey, I signed up for the Copper Mountain Rodeo at the end of this month. Maybe you'll come."

"The rodeo? I thought you gave that up."

"For a long time, I did. But I still have a few left in me."

"But bull riding isn't something you just pick up when you feel like it. After being gone from the sport for years."

"I've stayed in shape. I can still ride a bull."

Kate's gaze flicked to his arms again. She cleared her throat and took a deep sip of wine. "It's not the riding part that will kill you, it's the falling off part. It's the two thousand pounds of angry maniac pounding you into the ground or pulling you into the well and beating you to death. And you're not twenty-three anymore."

He leaned back with a grin. "Is that concern for my well-being?"

"What? *No.*" She fingered her wine glass. "All right. I may hate you, but that doesn't mean I want to see you get in some bull-riding wreck. Your children only have you. If you got hurt…"

"It's a considered risk. Everything in life is a risk, Kate. Everything. No risk, no real life."

She sat back. "I see. This is your philosophy? Risk everything? Damn the consequences? But I guess I should know that by now about you."

"Now we're talking about us?"

"If the shoe fits…"

"We were both wearing those shoes, Kate."

"What's that supposed to mean? You're blaming me for what happened?"

"No." This was the last direction he'd wanted to take this conversation in. "That was me. But there were two of us in that relationship, Kate. You were the one who insisted we take a break while you went to Florence for that semester abroad. *I* was the one who didn't want a break. I was the one who wanted to marry you. And then there was *Marcello.*" He could tell he shocked her with that name. "Oh, yeah. I know about him. Surprised?"

"Who told you about—?"

"Sharon. Your roommate. I ran into her on the street a few months later and she felt obliged to inform me about your side-of-Italian."

She bit back whatever she'd been about to say and shoved to her feet, heading to the couch where she'd left her things. "Okay. I knew this was a bad idea."

He got up and followed her. "Where you going?"

"Home."

"Just like that? You won't even talk about it?"

"Remind me to throttle Sharon Birch next time I see her." She pushed her arms into the sleeves of her jacket.

"But it's okay that *you* never mentioned him to me?"

She gulped and turned back to him. "Marcello…was nothing more than a—"

"—boyfriend?"

"No. We had a couple of innocent dates over there. He was…it turned out he was a jerk. If anything, meeting Marcello only solidified my feelings about you."

"Yeah? Well, I didn't date *anyone* while you were gone. Not one girl. Not until that night when I was drunk and Melissa was—"

"—a buckle bunny, hoping to hitch herself to your star?"

"*One night*. I never intended for…what happened to *happen*, but I didn't cheat on you, Kate. We were broken up."

"Maybe. But at least I didn't *sleep* with Marcello."

"We were *broken up.*"

"Until we weren't. Until I had a ring on my finger and we were planning our wedding. And she came up pregnant. And you *chose her.*"

A long, awful pause stretched between them. All the hurt and pain between them filled that terrible space, and he realized that neither of them had put the past behind them. Not any of it.

"I'd give anything not to have hurt you the way I did, Kate. But wishing changes nothing. I chose my child. My *children*, as things turned out. And yeah. No matter the consequences of marrying their mother, no child of mine would ever grow up the way I did. Without feeling loved and cared for by their father. And I'll never regret being their father or doing what needed to be done to protect them."

She shifted the things in her arms. "Like riding bulls again."

"Yes," he bit out a little defensively.

"And now, apparently, she wants them back."

He blinked. His turn to feel heat blossom on his face. "How could you know about—?"

"The court papers. The ones you left on your side table? I wasn't really snooping. I just happened to see them lying out there when you were upstairs putting the kids to bed. I am the daughter of an attorney. They caught my eye. And I know what they are. *Hong Kong?*"

The loose ends of him felt like they were unwinding like a fraying rope. But now that she knew, there was no undoing it. "I think she just wants to screw with me. That's become her life's ambition."

Silent, Kate waited for more. He shoved two hands through his hair. "After the kids were born, with me gone competing, she started to drink. She discovered early on that she didn't want kids after all, she wanted my undivided attention. She never gave a damn about them. She's the reason I gave up the rodeo, because she was incapable of caring for them."

Kate watched him now, her eyes turning a deep, dark green.

He went on. "She would leave them with babysitters and go out to party when I was out of town. Sometimes for days on end, though I didn't find that out until later. One day, I came home a day early to find her passed out on the couch and Cutter's little mouth bleeding from a fall or something that could have been so much worse. And that was my fault, for not seeing what was happening until almost too late.

"That day, I gave up the rodeo, the trips out of town. I tried to get her help, but she didn't want it. Because between us, Melissa and me? There was nothing but the twins holding us together. And that was the end for us, for her as a mother, for me with my bull riding career. She gladly signed away full custody and it's been me and them ever since. Until now. The kids, they don't even know her. They wouldn't know her if they passed her on the street."

Kate blinked back some emotion he couldn't name as she watched him. "I'm sorry."

"So," he said, "I need to settle. I need stability. I need to give my children the home they deserve. And yes, I'll risk everything to give that to them. More even. Because I owe them that. And I'll never let her take them."

Outside, the rain had stopped and a slow drip-drip-drip echoed outside the door. "So, you're going to fight her?"

"Yes. With everything I have. But keeping custody will be an uphill battle. Seems the court favors families and biological mothers, whether they abandon their children or not. So my attorney tells me. And I'm an unmarried, single dad who works too much." He stopped short, knowing he'd probably told her more than she'd wanted to hear. But when he looked up, her eyes had gone dark with some lurch of realization and she was glaring at him.

Backing up a step, she said, "Ohhh, no. Oh, no you don't."

He frowned. "What?"

She backed away from him. "Absolutely not! Is that what this whole evening has been about?" she demanded. "All leading up to this? That you need a 'wife' to parade in front of a judge?"

Her accusation roiled through him. "Of course not. Don't be ridiculous. No. This has nothing to do with you."

She blushed furiously, then headed to the door. "Good,

because you can forget it. That will never happen, Finn. Not in a million years. You know I hate you, right? I can't even believe you would consider such a thing."

"I didn't." *Until you mentioned it.* "But just for the record, if I were going to ask you for that kind of help...that kind of favor, I wouldn't have gone through the back door like that. I would have asked you straight out. That is, if I'd thought there was a chance in hell you'd do something like that for me."

She blinked back at him, something on the tip of her tongue to say before she changed her mind. "Well, I *wouldn't.*"

"And I didn't ask. Kate, stop. Where are you going?"

"I'm leaving."

"Wait a minute."

Her hand on the door knob, she turned on him. "No, *you* wait, you...you..." She gave a frustrated growl for lack of a more descriptive word. "That is just low. Telling me your sad story. Playing on my sympathies like that, so I'd feel sorry for you. I could just...just—"

"Just what? Punch me?" he asked, moving between her and the doorway. "Kiss me?"

"*Kiss* you? *As if!*" But her eyes had dilated to black splotches and a tremor ran down her as she backed up against the opened door. Her nostrils flared with anger, and her scent washed over him afresh.

"Punch me then. Or kiss me. Whatever makes you feel

better."

Hands splayed against the door behind her, she narrowed a look at him. "As I am not a violent person, I choose C. None of the above." But with the door wide open beside her, she wasn't choosing to exit either.

He braced a hand on the doorjamb beside her and loomed over her. "When was the last time someone kissed you 'til your knees stopped workin'? Huh? I used to be able to do that to you, remember?"

Oh, she was remembering. He could see the memory in her eyes.

"I—no, I don't recall that...and—" she flicked that red hair out of her eyes with a jerk of her head—"I'm leaving now." But her effort to go was merely a twitch in the direction of the car.

"Wow. That long, huh?"

She opened her mouth in silent outrage, but no words came to mind. No denial anyway.

In fact, right now, she looked as if a windstorm had just blown through all of her carefully nurtured self-righteousness. Finally, she stammered, "I've had plenty of kisses from plenty of men and I—"

"—men like Cree Malone, for instance? Is he a good kisser?"

She probably thought he didn't catch the wince, but he did.

"Plenty of men," she repeated. "Not that it's any of your

business. At all. And the last thing I need is a kiss from *you*."

"Really?" He took a step closer until their mouths were only inches apart. Until he could feel the pebbled nubs of her nipples brush against his shirt. "The *last* thing?"

She swallowed hard and moistened her lips with the tip of her tongue. "The very last thing," she reiterated, as he bracketed his hands beside her head there on the doorway and lowered his nose to her hair to inhale her scent. "Stop doing that."

"You smell really good," he murmured against her hair. "What *is* that?"

Clutching the wooden door behind her, she tipped her face away from him. "I'm warning you."

"Is that the same perfume you used to wear? Right here, wasn't it?" He dropped his mouth down to a spot below her ear, that place he remembered used to make her lose it. He nipped at that spot gently with his teeth and a quake rolled through her.

"Chanel," she breathed so quietly he almost missed it, and she tipped her head back against the door giving him access to more.

And not being a fool, he took the opportunity to slide his mouth along the ridge of her throat and up her jaw.

"I like it," he murmured, but in truth, he'd been hard all night for her and the close-up scent of her skin was like a drug. "You remember this, Kate? I do." He exhaled against her throat. "God, I do."

He took her face in his hands and pulled her to him, kissing her as if this would be the last time. His mouth slid against hers, taking, tasting what he'd wanted to taste all these years. She made a small sound of protest as she pushed against his chest, but a moment later, her fingers clutched his shirt and she relented, kissing him back. Her soft lips—oh, yeah, he'd never forgotten them—opened to his with unexpected hunger, and the door banged against the wall behind it. He tasted wine on her tongue and anger in the way hers did battle with his. But she flattened herself against him, wanting more.

He forgot the risks of touching her this way again, the years it had taken him to pull himself back from the loss of her last time. Because all he could think about now was how right they felt together after all these years. How perfectly right.

For a heartbeat, her arms went around his neck, then, just as quickly, fell away as if touching him that way had betrayed her restraint somehow. With his knee braced between her legs he felt her knees buckle slightly before she slapped her hands behind her to support herself against the door.

She broke the kiss. "Stop!" she breathed, breathless, turning her head away from him. "Stop doing that."

He tipped his forehead against her temple, breathing hard before he stepped back away from her, locking his thumbs in his back pockets so he wouldn't be tempted to touch her again.

She glared at him, her eyes filled with a myriad of emotions: accusation, raw hunger and confusion. And those were just the ones he understood.

He didn't try to explain himself. He let the kiss speak for itself.

She clapped a hand on his chest, a gesture halfway between a push and tug. And with a thousand arguments on the tip of her tongue, she was gone.

Chapter Three

THE KINDERGARTEN PLAYGROUND at school was separate from the larger playground and backed up to a fence that separated that yard from Main Street. Shaded by large trees and bordered by a grassy lawn, the climbing structures were crowded with children as Kate and her fellow teacher, Janice Brinker stood together, watching the shrieking children chase each other around the yard. Janice had a few years of teaching on Kate and was pretty in a girl-next-door kind of way. But she'd come from Chicago and dressed like a big city girl and Kate adored her.

"I heard," Janice told Kate, looking glum. "Bette Moynihan s coming back earlier than she expected. In two days? Wasn't your gig supposed to be until November?"

Kate nodded with a sigh. "It's a miracle. I guess her mother's broken leg healed faster than they thought."

"I'll miss you. So will they," Janice said, staring off at the children on the playground. "Unemployment sucks. Maybe they'll find you another spot in another classroom."

Kate sighed. "A day here and there, I suppose. But that's

not going to pay my rent."

"What will you do?"

"Apply elsewhere. Maybe another city. Maybe Missoula." She shrugged, leaning her head back to absorb some sun. "There's a whole dating pool there I haven't dipped a toe into for years."

Janice chuckled. "But leave Marietta? Your whole family is here."

Kate nodded, wondering if that wasn't part of the problem. "Maybe no one's meant to be in one place too long. Especially a town this small. This place is feeling a little crowded suddenly."

Cutter, wearing his neon-green cast, now covered with drawings and happy faces, darted around the swings, playing tag with two other boys. "You'd never guess that two nights ago, he was in the ER"

"Lucky he didn't break worse than his arm, from the sound of it," Janice said as they watched Cutter Scott collide with another boy in true Cutter fashion. The boys fell into a pile and rolled on the thick protective matting, laughing.

"*Boys*," Kate said.

"They will *be*," Janice agreed.

"What about Caylee?" Kate asked. "She seems...quiet." The child was sitting by herself in the sandbox drawing circles in the sand.

"She is. Sweet girl. But I think she's hungry for something. Female attention would be my guess. She's the only girl in a very male household, you know. All that testosterone…"

Yes, she knew. Her own pheromones were still tingling in reaction.

"Cutter's dad had just left a teachers' conference with me the other night when Cutter took his fall. I missed the whole thing. That was the first time I'd met him. He was, um, *nice*." Janice leaned against a concrete wall with a sigh. "And he'd give Charlie Hunnam a run for his money."

Kate shot a wide-eyed look at her.

"*What*? I'm married, not blind," Janice said with a chuckle. "I had to force myself not to gawk at him."

Kate grinned and looked away. She knew the feeling. But she wasn't ready to talk about Finn yet. She was hardly even ready to think about him. "You and a thousand other girls."

"*You* met him. You drove him to the hospital, I hear. You don't agree?"

She opened her mouth to answer, but one of the school secretaries, Mabel Kramer, poked her head out the door of Janice's classroom just then and called, "Phone call in the office for you, Janice. It's your husband. He says your cell is turned off."

Janice glanced down at her phone, which was, indeed, set on mute. "Darn! I'd better go call him. He's been waiting all week to hear about a promotion at work. You okay here for a couple of minutes alone?"

"Sure. Go on."

After Janice disappeared into her classroom, Kate took a stroll around the playground. The children weren't the only ones who loved this time of day. Kate appreciated the break and the warm September breeze that tugged at the nearby trees as her thoughts strayed to the man who had been barging into her mind like this for days.

She didn't need Janice to remind her about Finn Scott's uncanny effect on womankind. He didn't even have to try to look hot, which was, she supposed, part of his appeal. His sexiness was effortless and unaffected. Women simply couldn't help themselves around him. God knows, the other night, she couldn't.

She'd allowed him to breach her defenses. Big mistake. Big, big mistake. Case in point: the womanly parts of her that had ached for hours after she'd left.

For instance, just remembering that knee-buckling kiss—right now—caused her nipples to harden into tight little buds.

Stop that right now! Stop thinking about him!

She gave her long hair an irritated flick over her shoulder. *Think of something else. Think of Cree Malone and the tongue lashing he gave your cheek.*

Disturbingly, that worked.

Better.

She let out a breath. After all, she'd already allowed herself to lose several perfectly good nights' sleep over their little encounter the other night and the confusing way things had ended. Far better to nurture her anger with him than to allow those feelings to dissipate in a haze of unwanted lust.

And thoughts of his mouth sliding against her skin.

She blinked and throttled her thoughts. For all her hastiness, possibly jumping to wrong conclusions the other night, the problem, she decided, was that she needed closure. A once-and-for-all, get-him-out-of-your-heart kind of closure. Anyone who knew her well knew she wasn't a wrap-things-up-neatly kind of girl with men, and usually kept things light enough that no such messiness was required.

But if she were being honest, the *Kate* that never needed closure, the serial dater, the girl who inspired interventions, had evolved from the girl who still felt bruised by Finn's leaving six years ago. And deep down she feared that feeling of not being good enough might never go away.

Two five-year-olds darted in front of her, practically colliding with her and nearly took her out. "What speed do we use on the playground?" she called to them.

"Slow speed," they answered in one voice, and immediately put their heads together to conjure up more trouble.

"That's right..." Kate murmured, allowing her gaze to wander across the sun-warmed heads of the children to the nearby road.

That's when the car parked across the street caught her attention. The black town car had tinted windows that made it impossible to see inside. All but the back window, which was halfway down. Inside the car, an elegant-looking dark-haired woman wearing expensive dark glasses sat, her gaze pinned on Caylee. She looked like she might have gotten lost from a funeral procession, in her little black dress and as out of place in her town car on the streets of Marietta as a greyhound was at a rodeo.

Kate took a couple of steps toward the fence to get a closer look, which drew the woman's attention. She made eye contact with Kate for a long moment before she seemed to recognize her. And suddenly, Kate recognized her right back.

Melissa.

Finn's ex-wife in a town car, looking like she'd stepped off the pages of Vanity Fair. Kate had only seen her once, walking down the street in Missoula, months after she and Finn had broken up. She'd been minding her own business, when she'd practically walked into them on the sidewalk. Melissa had been very pregnant and Finn had his hand on the small of his wife's back, the way he once had done with her.

The three of them stopped short, right there on the street, speechless, frozen. *Awkward* didn't even cover the moment. She remembered him fumbling Melissa's name and Kate remembered wishing the sidewalk would swallow her up right there as the woman possessively tightened her arm around his. Kate had mumbled something about the weather, while Finn's expression thundered up like a dark cloud.

And then, the encounter was over. She moved on. So did they.

Until now.

But the woman in the town car? That was Melissa all right, though she looked nothing like the sad woman Finn had described the other night. The woman who had passed out on his couch and abandoned her children. This woman looked pulled together. Wealthy.

Arrogant.

Kate gripped the wrought iron fence in one hand and Melissa lifted her Audrey Hepburn chin in a little gesture of recognition, an unfriendly half-smile tilting her mouth. And then...and then she waved five fingers at Kate in a little '*take that, Bitch*' toodle-loo. The window rolled up and the town car pulled away, disappearing down the street.

Cold seeped into her, despite the warm day. *Oh, no, she didn't.*

But she had. *Girl, you have just messed with the wrong person.*

Somehow, Kate had imagined a fair fight between Finn and his ex. A fight that he could, and probably would, win. But this woman, this new version of Melissa, had landed, somehow, in a pile of money. And that, she feared, was very bad news for him. Money talked in a courtroom. Money that he didn't have.

Worse than that, even, was the possibility that this custody battle Melissa was about to wage on him, was just another game to her and had nothing to do with her wanting her children back. And everything to do with winning. And that possibility made her sick to her stomach.

"You're pale as a ghost, Kate. Are you all right?" Janice asked, appearing at her side.

No. Suddenly, she wasn't okay at all. She dragged her gaze away from the disappearing town car. "I'm just, um…warm. I'm just going to run in and grab a bottle of water. Did you get good news? The phone call?"

Janice's face lit up. "As a matter of fact, yes. He got the promotion. So proud of him. He couldn't wait 'til he got home to tell me."

Kate smiled, happy for her. What would her life be like with someone to share things with? Good things. Big and small things. The very idea seemed out of her sphere of reference. How many years had passed since she'd shared anything of herself with anyone, she wasn't even sure she remembered how.

Janice bumped Kate's arm affectionately. "I haven't given up on finding someone for you, you know."

Kate backed away from her, saying, "You always were a sucker for lost causes."

"…says the gorgeous redhead," Janice scoffed.

"Just to ease your matchmaker's burden, be advised that I'm on a dating hiatus. So, look no further. Men are off my list."

"Hey," she warned, with a straight face. "Don't get crazy on me, now."

"Thanks for the warning, but you may be too late."

She left Janice laughing as she ducked inside the class-room, digging her cell phone from her pocket. She dialed her attorney father's cell.

"Katydid!" She could hear the pleased smile in his voice. "To what do I owe the honor of a mid-day phone call? Everything all right?"

In the background, she could hear the bustle of what sounded like the courthouse. She'd caught him away from his office, which wasn't unusual. "Everything is just fine," she assured him. "I'm sorry to bother you. Do you have a second to talk, Daddy?"

"More than a second. Always. What's up?"

"Okay. I need your legal-eagle opinion on something. It's a Family Law matter. A custody case. I…um…" She hesitated, almost afraid to say what she was thinking out loud. "Do you know a judge up in Missoula named Corillo?"

FINN WAS KNEE deep in mud that afternoon, pulling a broken fencepost from a mud-filled hole when his cell phone rang. He didn't recognize the number, but it was local, so he pulled off one glove and answered. "Hello?"

Silence on the other end. "Hello?" he repeated.

"Just so you know," the very female voice on the other end said, "kissing me like that changes nothing."

Kate. His heart stuttered and he couldn't help the automatic grin that curved his mouth remembering that kiss.

And the way her arms slid around his neck. And her knees buckled. Most of all, he liked that he wasn't the only one still thinking about that kiss. "Okay," he said, waiting for more.

"And I still hate you."

That wasn't what he was hoping for. "Okay."

"Just so we're clear."

"Then why'd you call? And how'd you find my number? Not that I mind you did…"

"I have my ways. I just thought you should know, I saw your ex-wife earlier today. She was watching the kids on the school playground from across the street."

A shot of cold straightened his spine. *Damn the woman.* "You sure it was her?"

A pause stretched between them that he couldn't interpret. "Yes. I'm sure. She was in a town car. Looking very…well…let's just say she's not hurting at all for money."

Something inside him took a plunge. He should have known she'd land well. But what was she doing here in town? Stalking the kids? Trying to figure out how to contact them? Why didn't she just come to him? Or maybe she was watching Kate. She'd never gotten over her jealousy of her.

He blinked and stared down at the muddy hole he was standing in. He tugged his foot from the goo of the hole.

"What's that sound?" Kate asked.

"Mud. Winning."

"Oh."

An awkward silence stretched between them. A thousand

things filtered through his brain to say to her, but none of them managed to make the cut and find his tongue. He pictured her at the other end of the line, waiting for him to speak, and finding herself similarly speech challenged. He wondered if she was thinking about what he was thinking about. His lower half stirred at the thought.

"Carry on, then," Kate said at last. "I just thought you should know."

"Thanks. I…appreciate the heads up."

"All right then…"

Another pause, but she didn't hang up. "Kate?"

"Yeah?" she said quickly.

"Do you really hate me?"

Pause. "When the rational part of my brain is functioning," she said. "I mean…yes."

A smile edged the hard line of his mouth. He could almost hear her twirling her red hair around her finger, contemplating her next smart aleck retort. He glanced up at the sprawl of land surrounding him—his land—and wished she was standing beside him. "I've missed you, Kate."

"Oh, hey," she said, clearing her throat. "I'm getting another call. Gotta run."

"Okay. See you around?"

The next sound he heard was the dial tone.

THAT EVENING, KATE joined her step-mother, Jaycee, on a

sunset ride on her parents' ranchette, called Lane's End. With her father out of town on a deposition in Helena, she and Jaycee had saddled up two of her step-sister, Olivia's, gentlest horses and taken the trail through the north pasture toward the glassy smooth Yellowstone River.

It wasn't often that Kate rode anymore, even though, conveniently, Olivia ran a riding school out of her parents' stable. Riding here would always be easy to manage, but her life had gotten caught up in a relentless cycle of work, more work and the long string of men she'd wasted her spare time on dating these last few years. In fact, now that she thought about it, she'd spent very little time just enjoying this beautiful place.

Which felt, at this moment, like a crime.

"I like it here. The kids like it," Finn had said. Of course he did. What's not to like? She'd be hard pressed to find any country more beautiful than this. But sharing her hometown with Finn was another matter altogether.

Except for the phone call, she'd had no other contact with him since the other night, which had given her more than enough time to obsess over every twisty turn the evening had taken. More than enough time to realize that her accusations about him setting her up couldn't have been true. He couldn't possibly have known they'd end up at the ER that night, nor could he have planned to put those papers where she could accidentally find them. And if such a thing had, belatedly, occurred to him-that she had the potential to help him fight his ex-wife's custody case by fake-marrying him-she couldn't exactly blame him for that.

The kiss, on the other hand…she *could* blame him for that kiss. Even now, as she remembered how he'd teased her into that blunder with that irresistible smell of his, talking her down from the high horse she'd climbed up on with the nip of his teeth, while demolishing her perfectly good reasons for hating him by making her want him.

She *couldn't* want him.

But she did.

She'd lain awake, trying to imagine a life in Marietta, where they lived parallel lives that never intersected. But this valley was too small for that. Too small for both of them to share this place with all their unresolved 'feelings' still floating around like little predator drones, lying in wait to ambush them when they least expected it.

Seeing him again—kissing him—had made her itch for something she'd forgotten she'd ever wanted.

She'd have to be crazy to get in the middle of that fight he was about to wage with Melisssa. Or masochistic.

Or …*crazy*.

At least, that's what the sensible right side of her brain was saying. The left side, the side that chronically had her rubbing shoulders with fallen angels, assigning a time stamp on men's shelf-lives and was generally occupied contemplating her next scathingly brilliant debacle, was currently up to no good at all, thinking about saving Finn and his children from 'that woman.'

She'd consulted, hypothetically, with her father about the situation and, knowing that particular judge, he'd agreed, in theory, with Finn's attorney. About everything. Not that that had surprised her. Her father had only confirmed the trouble Finn was about to step into alone.

None of this was her problem. If they hadn't run into each other, she'd still be blithely unaware of his predicament. But she wasn't, and she couldn't stop thinking about him. About them. About her own pathetic attempt to forget him with a string of losers who couldn't hold a candle to him.

She wasn't in love with him. No, that had ended long ago. Whatever she felt for him could be summed up in two words—*animal attraction*. Because, despite everything, he could still make her burn and hate herself for that weakness later.

That would pass. Just as such feelings did with every other man she'd ever dated. Finn's sell-by date had expired years ago and to stir up anything between them now would only be rehashing the good after the bad.

Wouldn't it?

She sighed up at the peachy clouds that tinged the darkening blue sky ahead as she and Jaycee picked their way down a trail to the river where the horses could take a drink. Even now, the early September evening was still warm. They'd talked little on the ride and Kate knew that was Jaycee's way of giving her the space she needed to figure out how to broach whatever topic had brought her here this evening.

After Kate's own mother had died when she and Eve were still young, Jaycee and her daughter, Olivia, had come along a few years later, like a bright wish, to save them all from sadness. But Kate's issues around secrets had started long before that, though, when she'd decided not to burden her father or Eve with things that might bring them sadness, to layer atop the loss all of them felt. And despite the fact that she could always count on Jaycee to listen and be a sounding board for them all, as the years passed, she found herself more and more protective of that happiness they'd managed to find. Which, in turn, mutated into an unhealthy tendency toward keeping secrets.

It was a problem she'd managed to mostly ignore until Finn came back. Now, it just felt...lonely.

At the river, they dismounted and let the horses drink and graze, simply ground tying them so they wouldn't stray. She and Jaycee stretched out the kinks, then perched on a granite overhang and stared out across the valley. In the distance, the low profile of Marietta skimmed the horizon. To the east, the craggy Beartooth Mountains fingered up into the blue and the tips disappeared in low clouds.

"Did you ever think you'd end up here?" she asked Jaycee. "When you were younger?"

"Here, as in *here*? Or as in living the life I'm living?"

"Yeah," Kate answered with a smile. "How did you know

what choice was right for you?"

"I suppose when I was still married to Olivia's father, I couldn't have imagined this life. I'd made choices and thought I was just stuck with them. Turns out, I wasn't."

"I've always thought you were brave. That you must always have been brave."

Jaycee shook her head, her long salt and pepper hair shining in the sun. "I became brave. I took my life back. My first husband...Olivia's father, well...we were a bad match. When I finally got nerve enough to leave him, your father, who'd been widowed a few years already, gave me a job and the rest, as they say, is history. I just knew when I met him that he was the right choice for me. I fell in love with him and I just knew."

Kate shook her head and plucked a piece of nearby bluestem grass and stuck it between her teeth. "But taking us all on as a package...my dad and Eve and me, I mean, that could have been awful. I've heard stories."

"So had I," she admitted. "But I couldn't have asked for more than you girls gave me and each other. You were easy to love. No bravery involved. And don't forget your father's part. He gave Olivia his name and raised her as his own. I couldn't have asked for a better father for her, or for you girls, for that matter. We're all very lucky, I think."

The river burbled by with a steady hum. Nearby, the comforting sound of the horses cropping up tufts of grass mingled with the rusty songs of the redwing-blackbirds as they chased bugs along the surface of the water. Beneath her hands, the granite still held the warmth of the day, but Kate had felt cold for days and she couldn't shake the chill.

"What is it?" Jaycee asked, touching Kate's hand. "Is something bothering you?"

"I…" she began, then took a deep breath. "I never told you about…someone."

Those grey eyes sharpened. "Who?"

"A boy from college. I don't know why I never told you, told any of you. To be honest, I wasn't really planning to tell you about him now. I don't know why I am."

"Because you're ready to, I suppose."

Kate brushed her hair from her eyes, thinking of the way he'd looked at her and how incorrigible she'd been in return. "I was in love with him once. But…I guess I couldn't quite believe my good luck, even then. I kept him a secret. From everyone."

"Oh. *Kate*…" She squeezed her hand.

"I know. And I know *you* know what Olivia and Eve did last weekend. I know they had your full approval."

"I wouldn't go that far, but they did tell me their concerns. We've all been a little worried about you."

"Well, they weren't right to get in the middle of my messed up life," Kate said, "But I don't think they were exactly wrong either."

"Which is why you're telling me this now?"

"No. I'm telling you now because… he's here. That boy

I loved once. Not a boy anymore. At all. I saw him the other day." She told her about the ER debacle and the dinner after. "It wasn't a date. He invited me over to thank me for helping them."

"Not a date," Jaycee said with a smile, marking the distinction down in an imaginary note-to-self. "Is he…still married?"

Kate shook her head. "Divorced."

"And so…?"

"And so *nothing*. The night ended weirdly." Her edit button on how *exactly* that night had ended was firmly in place. "But, that wasn't exactly a surprise. That's pretty much money in the bank where men and I are concerned. What surprised me was how hurt he looked when I admitted I'd never told anyone about him. We dated for almost a year."

"You didn't tell anyone because…?"

"I don't know." Kate stared at the river sliding by and the rocks visible below through the crisp, clear water. How long had they been there, those rocks? And did they move or had they been planted there for centuries? She glanced up at her step-mom. "Okay, that's not true. I told him I'd kept our relationship a secret because I was afraid to jinx what we had. But now, I don't think that was the reason. I don't think I trusted what we had and I didn't want to be caught making a huge mistake. Or admitting it to you guys. Turns out, making mistakes is practically a calling with me."

"Ahh. That's not true and you know it. And, besides, there are worse things, you know, than mistakes," Jaycee said, patting her hand.

"There's never learning from them…" Kate propped her elbows on her knees and scraped her hair back from her face with two hands and a sound of frustration. "I mean, I push people away. Men. Like…I'm afraid of anything good. The old, 'I ditch them before they can ditch me,' conundrum. Except for him, of course. That was the other way around."

Jaycee shook her head in the way she did when she knew arguing with that kind of logic was illogical. "And how's that working for you, darling?"

Kate sighed. "Not well."

"So, he's here now…why?"

"Apparently, he inherited Frank Greevy's old place. But I could have something to do with his decision to stay in Marietta."

"You could always ask him."

"I don't think we really tell each other the truth any-more." She lifted her gaze to the woman who'd never steered her wrong, despite years of Kate believing that she knew better. "I don't know what to do."

"Do?"

"He might need my help."

Jaycee sighed, brushing dust off her jean-covered thighs. "Do what your heart tells you to do. That's the fun of it, Kate. Choosing. This, and not that. That, and not this? And if you make a choice, and you don't like where it's going, change it. It's only when we stand still that we really fail. Because, Katie, choosing is all we have."

FINN HAD PROMISED the twins a special dessert at the Main Street Diner for their date night if they finished up their chores. Deprived as they were by a father who had no baking talents, they finished their chores in record time. So after a home cooked meal, they took an evening ride to the diner.

There, the hostess, a pretty, high-school girl named Emily, escorted them to an empty booth along the wall. The Main Street Diner, run by Paige Joffe, had been a fixture in Marietta for years and boasted hand-made desserts and kid-friendly food and he'd often eaten there when coming into town for coaching by his mentor, Frank Greevy.

A pang of sadness struck him as he remembered the man. An old bull-rider himself from the old days, Frank had coached some of the best bull-riders out there. He lived alone, never married and considered his boys family. Cancer had taken him after a long battle and Finn was certainly not the only rider to come back to visit him. He'd died surrounded by friends. Not in a million years did he ever expect the gift Frank had left him and he would be forever grateful to the man for thinking enough of him to leave him his precious land.

And someday, this place would belong to his children.

"What's your pleasure, you two?" he asked once they'd settled into their places and cracked open the crayons and children's menus. "Sundaes? Cupcakes? Apple pie?"

The kids crowed their answers simultaneously.

"Cupcake!"

"Sundae!"

Then, for good measure, they shouted, "Miss Candy!"

Finn froze as Cutter waved his casted arm at someone apparently sitting directly behind him, then started crawling across the table in greeting. He held out a staying hand and half-turned to look.

And there she was. *How had he missed that red hair of hers?*

Kate turned in her seat and tipped a small smile at the twins and him. He felt his stomach take a tumble at the sight of her. She had her hair up in a clip and was wearing her work clothes, a short-sleeved blue thing that made her eyes look a smoky grey-green.

With a half-eaten salad beside her, she had her laptop open to what looked like a Craigslist of job listings. She shut the laptop with a snap and he swallowed thickly, bracing himself for her to get up and walk away again in a rush of frigid air.

"So," she said, in a voice more welcoming than he'd expected. "We meet again."

"I guess Marietta is a smaller town than I thought."

"Come and sit with *us*, Miss Candy? There's room,"

Caylee beseeched her. Cutter heartily agreed and slid over to make space for her on their side. "We're having a special dessert!"

Finn held his breath, expecting a *no*, but she was apparently waiting for him to extend the invitation himself. He gestured to the seat beside the kids and said, "Please."

After a moment's hesitation, she gathered up her purse, laptop and food, and changed booths, sliding in beside Caylee, who wrapped an arm around Kate's in a sweet hug.

"So, what's the special occasion?" she asked the twins.

"It's our date night," Caylee said, matter-of-factly. "With Daddy because we have a new ranch. And because he can't make cupcakes."

"And we did all of our chores," Cutter added.

Kate's eyes flicked up to his and caught him grinning at his daughter.

"Date night? That *is* special," Kate said.

Breathlessly, the kids launched into a description of what they would do with all that space at the ranch, and how they decided to share a room, even though they each had one. With wide-eyed fascination, Kate listened to every word, intermittently glancing at Finn, who could not take his eyes off her, or get over how smitten his children seemed to be with her.

He motioned to the waitress and quietly ordered for them as they got to the part about the cow they'd petted on the Double G Ranch this afternoon where he'd been negotiating for a bull, and described, in detail, the definition of *chewing cud.*

"Kind of like this?" she asked, chewing a bite of her own food, then mooing for them. That earned her a roar of giggles.

"But you need hay," Cutter said and Kate lifted her hands helplessly.

Dessert arrived and, like magic, the children fell silent, digging into their sweet treats. Finn, who had gotten a hot fudge sundae, dug beneath the whipped cream for a bite of chocolate.

She smiled up at him. "I'm glad we ran into each other," she said, pushing salad around on her plate.

"Really? Me, too." He was. He just wasn't sure if he should be ducking or not. She might want to make good on that punch.

"I don't know if you heard, but the teacher I'm subbing for is coming back early. Tomorrow, in fact. So, I suddenly find myself officially out of work."

Hence, the job site on her laptop. "They're crazy to lose you."

"Stuff happens," she said with a twitch of regret in her smile.

"So what'll you do now?"

She shrugged. "I'll have to apply elsewhere. The budget here in Marietta has tightened up. I'll look out of town, I guess."

Disappointment tightened his jaw. Just as he was getting here, she was leaving.

"But…in the meantime," she began, "to be honest, I've done a lot of thinking about the other night at your place."

Here comes the boom. "Really?"

"Yes. You cooked such a nice meal," she said, meaningfully, glancing sideways at the kids who were watching the exchange, with sudden interest. "And I was thinking how sometimes, you leave things on your *plate* you wish you *hadn't.*"

"Uh-huh," he said, trying to follow along. She had left food on her plate.

"And maybe you were a little hasty. And you didn't even get to the dessert. You know what I mean?"

He squinted at her. Cutter nodded his agreement as he ate. "Daddy doesn't make dessert."

"Well, why don't you get one?" Caylee asked, looking up with frosting on her nose.

"You're absolutely right, Caylee. I will." She snagged their waitress and pushed the remains of her salad away. "I'd like one of those, please," she said, indicating Finn's sundae. But to him, she said, "Because *sometimes*, a little *chocolate* is in order."

"A little chocolate is *always* in order, in my opinion," he said warily, delaying scooping a bite of his confection in his mouth. "You…want a bite of mine while you wait?"

She stared at him through a sweep of dark lashes as if she

were trying to decide. But the moment stretched beyond a simple bite of chocolate sundae. She glanced pointedly at his children. "What I'm saying is…I *might*," she suggested, finally, stealing a small bite from his sundae, "be able to assist you with the dessert you made—" she eyed Cutter and Caylee pointedly—"*temporarily,* that is. Just until the *waiter* in Missoula decides who gets which dessert."

He handed her his spoon, glancing at his children who were happily wolfing down their sugary treats. His heart suddenly started pounding against his ribs. "*What?*"

"You see, I've given this a lot of thought, since I saw you last. About how some recipes can be accidentally messed up. You know, like when you should have added sugar but you added salt, instead?"

He nodded.

"Take cupcakes, for instance." She slid her gaze again to the twins. "In the hands of the right baker, they can be so delicious. Everyone wants them. But sharing cupcakes can be difficult. If not downright impossible. Right?"

"Right!" Caylee agreed, scooting her plate away from Cutter.

He nodded, feeling heat crawl across his skin.

"And bad for the cupcakes, too," she said. "Since cupcakes are so small and have no say over who gets to keep them."

Caylee studied her half-eaten cupcake in a new light, then took another bite.

"So, you're saying," he began, slowly, "that the baker might be able to keep his cupcakes with the help of someone who had a fondness for his particular cupcakes."

With an exaggerated nod, she handed him back his spoon. "*Yeeess*. A fill-in assistant baker, so to speak, to stand up for those cupcakes. Solely for their sake, of course. And only until she knew they were safe with the baker who had already worked so hard to make them."

Finn leaned back in his seat, his heart in his throat. "But why would she do that—this assistant fill-in baker...for him?"

With a shrug, Kate said, "In the interest of fairness. And because she's in between bakeries?" The waitress delivered her hot fudge sundae. She pulled the cherry off the top and popped it in her mouth. Around the delicacy, she added, "And because maybe she's not really as nice as the first baker thinks. Her motives might have something to do with...well, *payback* for the third baker. For barging into her kitchen uninvited." She smiled sweetly at him.

"Seriously?"

"Oh. She never jokes about dessert. Of course, that's only if the baker truly wants her help. Through the front door."

A disbelieving smile spread across his mouth. What she was offering, out of the blue, was nothing he could have imagined or anticipated and the reality of that stung his eyes. For the first time in days, he felt like he could breathe.

He leaned forward and braced his forearms on the table,

knowing he was agreeing to venture into unknown waters by way of a questionable vessel. But he didn't care. He'd take help any way he could get it. "I know for a fact that the baker would certainly and gratefully accept for the sake of his special cupcakes."

"All right then. Done." She took another bite of her sundae with a smile he couldn't quite interpret. This Kate, this self-contained Kate who seemed to run hot and cold about him, was a mystery he wanted solved. He couldn't get a handle on her or what her motives really were for helping him. Of course, he wanted to believe her willingness to help came from wanting to resolve their differences and find her way back to him. But simple had never been her M.O. And over time, she'd only gotten more complicated. Whether or not, in the short month he had, he could change her heart about him, one thing he knew for sure—his children would be safe with her.

Cutter, who had found the bottom of his sundae, suddenly shifted his gaze between the two adults with a questioning look. "Who is this baker, anyway?"

Chapter Four

B EFORE SHE COULD think better of what they were about
to do, or decide it was the craziest thing she'd ever
done, she drove with Finn to the courthouse in Bozeman—
far away from prying eyes in Marietta—on Friday morning.

After securing a marriage license, they were told to wait
outside the judge's chambers and, in between divorce
proceedings, in-chamber arguments and basically, whenever
he had time, he would marry them.

A crushing blow to romantics everywhere.

Except that Finn had secreted in white Calla lilies for her
to hold. Elegant, white flowers that reminded her of that
time in Missoula when he'd left them on her doorstep, the
morning after a fight. She was touched and at the same time
shocked that he remembered the Calla lily was her favorite
flower.

She'd worn a filmy summer dress she'd pulled out of her
closet and he'd put on a dark suit that looked like it had been
tailored to fit his sigh-worthy shoulders and chest. Except for
his too-long dark hair that curled around his collar, he didn't

look like a cowboy right now. In fact, if Tom Ford happened by, she suspected Finn would be snatched up to grace some billboard somewhere that would get city girls swooning.

She did her best not to stare, but found her gaze drifting back to the way his trousers hugged the muscled contours of his thigh where it brushed against her knee and the way his thumb wore a circle into the palm of his other hand. Despite the cool air conditioning inside the courthouse, Kate resisted the temptation to fan herself in response.

Just nerves. Or the smoldering hotness sitting beside her, trying hard to act like getting married on the spur of the moment under false pretenses was no big deal. For that matter, she was doing the same, less successfully.

They'd talked on the way up, setting the rules and agreeing that the children should know nothing of the upcoming hearing or about their mother's part in it. Nor would they know about this marriage. For their sakes, Kate would pose as a nanny, there to temporarily care for them. Then, when she left, there would be no hurt feelings, no issues of abandonment, of which they'd already had more than their fair share. They'd agreed that this whole marriage farce was solely for that crazy-ass judge up in Missoula who had a prejudice against single fathers and to even up the unfair advantage Melissa had brought to the playing field.

As straightforward as the whole thing sounded, nothing was as uncomplicated as saying yes that afternoon in the diner had been. Marriage to Finn, phony though it would be, was going to be messy and risky. And she wasn't even talking about legalities.

But here they were. For better or worse.

The courthouse was abuzz with activity. Jurors lingered nearby, attorneys walked in pairs, or alone, on their cells, discussing cases. Across the narrow hallway, a parolee sat with his mother next to the young couple that had been in line behind them for a license. Those two sat making eyes at one another and occasionally making out. They couldn't seem to keep their hands off each other.

Kate rolled her eyes at the ceiling. She felt old, just being in the same room with them, so she'd purposefully averted her eyes from them.

"Nervous?" she asked Finn.

He stopped rubbing his palm and pressed his hands together. With a reassuring smile, he answered, "You?"

"I won't lie. I feel like I just swallowed the scales of justice," she said, pulling her hair away from her face. "Comingling with all of these attorneys, I'm reminded that we're about to perjure ourselves with the *until death us do part* bit."

"You can still change your mind….about that part. You could play nanny without the marriage certificate. Maybe that would be enough stability in the eyes of the judge."

"You don't believe that."

He rubbed his palm again. "No."

"And, just so we're clear, we're agreed to an annulment

after the hearing. No arguments. No messy divorce."

A shrug that looked more like a cracking of his neck shifted his shoulders. "I gave you my word. And you stay until after the hearing."

She nodded and fidgeted in her seat. She tapped her foot on the smooth marble floor, then turned to him. "Do you think this is crazy?"

Turning those calm-in-a-storm eyes of his on her, he said, "Absolutely."

Stricken, she said, "Really?"

"But for my kids," he told her, "I'd do crazy all day long."

Swallowing back a lump of something she could only identify as sentimentality, she said, "I know."

Stick to the plan. The impulsive, very flawed plan. They were *doing* this for the twins. For their future good. Even as she'd reminded herself that she was marrying him partly to pay back Melissa for royally screwing with her life, now that she knew how wrong it had all gone, she gave less than two figs about Melissa. Shocking to discover that, except for feeling protective about Finn's children—and about him— all she wanted from Melissa was to curl up and…disappear.

He had apparently watched all of these thoughts cross her expression and for the first time since they'd arrived, concern creased his brow. "No, really. You want to call the whole thing off?"

"No," she answered quickly, so she wouldn't change her

mind. "Do you?"

He shook his head. "I'm grateful, Kate."

"Maybe you should thank me after this is all over. If you still want to."

"Finnegan Ray Scott and Katherine Louisa Canaday?" intoned the clerk from the judge's chamber doorway.

Finn stood and she shot to her feet beside him, trying to conceal her twitching hand behind the lilies.

"Last chance to change your mind," he whispered close to her ear.

She shook her head resolutely. "Let's just get this over with."

"Aw, Honey, that's so romantic," he said, loudly enough for the clerk to hear. He touched the small of her back with his hand, sparking a cavalcade of reactions up the column of her spine. Not the least of which involved her heart misplacing itself in her throat and every female nerve coming to full attention.

"Don't call me 'Honey,' *Finnegan*,'" she warned quietly, scooting just out of reach. "And keep your tongue to yourself when they pronounce us married."

He grinned as they entered the chambers. "As you wish."

Judge Hiltern must have repeated this ceremony some 23,674 times and his delivery did nothing to disguise that fact. He dispensed with the formalities quickly in his black robe and wire-rims, holding his Bible beneath the photo of the late Ronald Reagan shaking hands with him. Absently,

Kate wondered how much he'd had to pay at the plate dinner for that handshake. If he was in a rush, he'd learned to moderate his voice to hide it, but there was no shilly-shallying in the ceremony. No fluff. Just the facts.

After saying their "I do's," which they both managed without flubbing, he asked if there were rings to be exchanged.

"No, Your Honor," Kate piped up. "We don't actually believe in—"

"Yes, Your Honor," Finn said, cutting her off as he pulled something from the inside pocket of his jacket. "I have a ring." He produced a sparkling, radiant-cut diamond ring set in a platinum, diamond-wrapped band. A ring that looked all too hauntingly familiar.

Kate gasped. "Wh-what is that?"

"A ring."

"I—I see it's a-a—" she stammered, "but…is that the—?"

"Yup," he answered, that dimple in his left cheek making an appearance. "It is." He reached for her fingers. "Your hand?"

She felt like Julia Roberts in *Pretty Woman*, when Edward nearly snapped the blue velvet jewelry box on her fingers. Shocked. Surprised. *Gobsmacked.* She swallowed the nervous bark of laughter that nearly erupted from her.

This was the ring she'd thrown at him that day, the one that had made a sparkly, final sound as it found its accidental way into a ceramic bowl across the room and did a death spiral there. *This* was the ring she assumed had graced his wife's hand after he'd dumped Kate. Because who could afford another ring like this one, for wife number two?

But he'd kept her ring. In its box. All these years. And he had a wedding band to match.

So unfair to ambush her this way. But she had loved this ring and every promise attached to it. So much.

This marriage is only temporary, she wanted to shout at him. *I do not love this ring any more, and I do not love you!*

But he watched her with that gaze that she'd once trusted, waiting for her to give him her hand. Make a choice. Say yes.

The judge had been witness to hundreds of such coupling, both good and bad, and she could almost imagine him anticipating the thud of failure in their future.

So, against every lick of common sense she owned, she proffered her hand and let him slide that once-upon-a-time ring on her finger. It fit perfectly, of course. And yet, it fit not at all.

"And having both exchanged solemn vows and exchanged tokens of your fidelity and affection, then by the power vested in me by the State of Montana," Judge Hiltern said, "I now pronounce you husband and wife."

Finn's hands found hers across the ocean of distance between them and held them. Hers were suddenly cold and twitchy as fireflies trapped in a jar, but his firm, warm touch—against all reason—calmed her.

"And," the judge urged, clapping his Bible closed, "you may now kiss the bride." The witnesses, two court clerks, smiled patiently, waiting. She could demur, or turn her cheek at the last moment, but decided against it. They both had their parts to play.

He leaned forward and touched his lips to hers. A mere brush, at first, warming her fractionally, and then he reached a hand behind her head and slipped his fingers into her hair, pulling her to him. The second kiss made her remember why she couldn't forget him: his sweet taste, the heated softness of his lips and all the kisses they'd shared once. And, of course, the one on his doorstep.

He kept the kiss chaste and didn't press her to open to him, as he had the other night, but he left no doubt—with that one heart-pounding slide of his mouth against hers— that if he had a choice in the matter, there would be more.

Off-balance by the kiss, Kate blinked and pulled away, only to find him smiling at her. She sent a nervous smile back thinking, *What have I done?*

The two witnesses politely shook their hands, offering them congratulations and the judge followed suit.

"You two look as if you could stand a chance in this lottery called marriage," he told them. "See that you both put forth the effort required to succeed."

"We will," Finn said, blatantly lying to the face of justice. "Thank you, Your Honor."

THEY COULDN'T GET out of that courthouse fast enough. Grabbing her by the hand, Finn pulled her with him toward the pick-up they'd parked in the lot. When they hit the road, he opened the windows and sped down the highway in the opposite direction from Marietta.

"Wait. Where are we going? Home is that way," she pointed out, but he just smiled. She leaned back and braced an elbow on the door. "So, you're kidnapping me?"

"Oh, yeah. But only temporarily."

She studied his profile and the wicked little grin he couldn't contain.

"I knew you'd be trouble."

Early September heat bore down on the asphalt road and made the air simmer around them. From the flat prairie nearby, the wind carried the scent of summer-toasted sweet grass and whipped Kate's hair in an auburn froth around her face until she caught it in one hand.

While Kate watched him like he'd lost his mind, he put on one of her favorite tunes, Richie Haven's Woodstock acoustic anthem, *Follow* on his iPod and threw one arm out the window to catch the wind and sing along. "*...and maybe you can sing to me the words I just told you...if all the things you feel ain't what they seem... Then don't mind me 'cause I ain't nothin' but a dream.*"

She smiled back at him through a sweep of lashes, perhaps remembering, as he was, the days when music was a thread between them, when they used to lose their inhibitions on the backroads of Missoula together singing out loud. When even the worst of days could be made better with music. She'd introduced him to this song. *Follow* had been one of her parents' favorites and then, the song became one of hers. After a moment, she leaned her head back and laughed, reaching out her window to catch the wind, too.

"*Let your mind go reeling out and let the breezes blow you…*" he sang. "*…that maybe when we meet and suddenly I will know you…*"

"*….Then don't mind me 'cause I ain't nothin' but a dream*," she belted out with him at the next chorus and the wind caught their voices and swallowed them. "*And you can follow…*"

When the song ended, she said 'play it again,' and he did. This time they both sang along with every verse. He loved the unselfconscious way she sang even when she didn't hit all the notes perfectly. The way she laughed and stuck her head outside the window to shout the song into the wind. The ring on her left hand sparkled in the late afternoon sun as she danced in the seat beside him with her eyes closed. And the day's tension seemed to leak out of them.

They hardly passed a single car on the road, but they weren't going far. A few miles down the road to a place he knew. And by the time they'd sung that song and a couple of others he pulled into the parking lot of a small place, tucked back away from the road called McConnells. If they were a little early for dinner, he didn't care. He wasn't taking her home without feeding her and lifting a glass to the wheel they'd set in motion.

Inside the small, converted roadhouse was an unexpectedly chic restaurant that he'd heard had a fabulous chef and a waiting list weeks long. But not today. Today, the manager, an elegant woman of fifty-something, welcomed them by name as they walked in and seated them in a private booth in the back, already set with two glasses of champagne, a bowl of exotic olives and a plate of bruschetta.

The rest of the place was packed with diners and the white-jacketed servers moved with soundless precision from table to table in pairs, upholding McConnells's reputation for stellar service.

Dazzled, her body still visibly humming from their car ride, Kate just shook her head with a pleased smile, lifted her glass and clinked his.

"How did you do this? And on such short notice?" she asked. "This place is impossible to get into. I've heard this chef is incredible."

"I told them I was coming here with you and they suddenly had an opening." He grinned at her from across the table.

"*Hunh.* I think your nose is growing." She glanced at her left hand. "And while we're on the subject of sneaky...about this...*ring...*"

"It's your ring. It's always been yours."

"Finn…" she began, shaking her head.

"Let's not get bogged down with details. I wanted you to have them. Whether you wear the rings or not is up to you."

She took a sip of champagne and the diamond sparkled in the light. "I don't need to remind you we're just pretending, right? And that this ring could pay for more than a few prize bulls on your ranch."

He watched her over the rim of his glass. "Nope."

The bruschetta was calling and after they took the edge off their hunger, ordered food and some good red wine, he began to relax.

"Question," Kate said, drawing a circle on the tablecloth with her finger.

"Shoot."

"Tell me where you've been the last few years," she said. "Because I know you weren't in Marietta."

"Up in Missoula, mostly. But the last two years we've moved a few times. I've been working ranches in Boise, Helena and down in Denver, trying to learn the business from the ground up. Been lucky enough to work for some mentors who've been willing to teach me."

She traced the shape of her champagne flute with her finger. "I'll admit I was a little prickly the first night we met. But I had no right to complain about you settling here. And I can hardly argue against the place I love most. It's a great place to raise a family."

He tipped his head gratefully as the waiter delivered the

wine.

"That doesn't, by the way, mean I'm not prickly anymore," she said quietly, when the waiter left. "I am. Very prickly."

"What's a rose without a few thorns?" He popped an olive in his mouth and grinned.

"There, see? Don't go trying to sweet talk me, Finn Scott. That won't change anything."

He wondered if she was right about that. He hoped not. She stirred those old feelings in him without even trying. Feelings he'd numbed himself to years ago. He wanted to reach over and pull her closer. Run his thumb along the inside of her wrist and follow the path with his mouth. Leave a trail of dampness like a brand against her skin.

But only a lie of convenience bound them together now. What was underneath was too fragile to support any expectations. If he was smart, he'd keep the complication of him and Kate out of what he was trying to do. She'd made her feelings clear. He was grateful to her and maybe that would have to be enough.

Then again, maybe he was kidding himself.

"While we're on the subject of how this will work, I've drawn up a list of rules." She pulled a piece of paper from her purse and unfolded it.

He stared suspiciously at the paper. "Rules?"

She dipped a look in his direction. "To avoid any possible misunderstandings. You know…"

Picking up a piece of bruschetta, he stuffed it into his mouth and leaned back. "Go on."

"First, I keep my apartment. I'll move in with you, ostensibly, until after the hearing, but I'll keep my things where they are. That will make things easier in the end."

He took a sip of wine and signaled her to go on.

"Second, we don't share a room. Or a bed. No sleeping together. For all intents and purposes, I'm the nanny and we don't want any confusion."

He didn't like this rule, but he wasn't surprised by it. As far as confusion went, he wondered if she was talking about the kids or herself? Or maybe him?

"Third, no kissing. We all know where that leads."

He frowned. "Well, maybe just—"

"Fourth, we've already talked about the annulment. That's a given."

Not in his book. He'd do everything in his power to change her mind on that front. But if things came to that—

"And fifth, we don't tell anyone. Especially my family." She chugged a gulp of wine. "They wouldn't understand. Any talk about this marriage will take place in the courtroom in Missoula and no one here needs to know anything about it."

"*Kate?*" The all too familiar female voice came from somewhere behind her. She whipped around to find Olivia standing a few feet behind her, beside her tall dark and handsome fiancé, Jake Lassen, who was smiling.

Her sister, however, was not.

Chapter Five

"OLIVIA!" WIDE-EYED, KATE crumpled the paper in her hand and leapt to her feet. "What are you doing here?"

"I could ask you the same thing," Olivia said under her breath as she reached a hand across the table to Finn, who had just gotten to his feet. "I'm Olivia Canaday, Kate's older sister. This is my fiancé, Jake Lassen. And you're—?"

"Finn Scott. Nice to meet you, Olivia, Jake." He slid a look at Kate, who seemed like she was about to hyperventilate.

"Not the pro-bull rider, Finn Scott?" Olivia said.

"Uh, yeah. The same," he answered, taking Jake's proffered hand. That answer earned Kate a second, more probing look from her sister.

"No kidding?" Jake said. "Hey, really nice to meet you."

"Right. Well, you know it's always a treat to see you both. But we were just about to have dinner, so…" Kate said in a voice several octaves higher than normal, giving her sister a little nudge toward the door.

"With your….*date*," Olivia added, with a meaningful tip of her head that Finn couldn't interpret.

"What? Finn?" Kate laughed. "A date? No. He's not a date. This isn't a date. Right, *Finn*?"

"Not exactly," he agreed, feeling the slip and slide of dangerous territory moving beneath his feet. "No."

Olivia's confused gaze went back and forth between them.

That's when her eyes went wide as they fell to the sparkling diamond ring set on her sister's hand. She tried to speak, but no sound came out. For a moment, Finn feared she might be choking.

"It's—it's not what you think," Kate managed quickly, twisting her hand behind her back.

"It's. *Not*?" Horrified, Kate's sister pinned her attention on Finn, waiting for an explanation.

Oh, he wasn't about to step into this sisterly minefield.

Jake, having missed the sparkly culprit, must have sensed an oncoming crisis and put his arm around Olivia. "We didn't mean to interrupt you two. Just getting into this place is a bear. We've had reservations for months. Liv, darlin', let's leave them to their—"

"Jake?" Olivia said evenly, disengaging his arm, "why don't you sit here with *Finn* for a minute while Kate and I go powder our noses?"

"*No.*" Kate dug in her feet. "We don't need to powder our noses. I don't even have powder. Who uses powder anymore? Why don't we just talk about this later, *O-livia*? We're in the middle of a nice—"

"I'll tell you why. Because *later* might be too late." She took Kate's arm. "C'mon, you."

IN THE RESTROOM, they found themselves thankfully alone. Olivia paced back and forth in front of the large mirrors in the elegant lounge. "Please, do *not* tell me that you just married a stranger, Kate."

Hands on her hips, Kate glared at her and said, "Okay."

"You have *got* to be kidding me. Barely a week ago, you promised us you wouldn't even date for a month! Now this?"

"I'm not dating." She turned and stared at her reflection in the mirror. "I'm *married*."

Olivia put her fingers in her ears and sang, "La-la-la-la-lah!"

Kate rolled her eyes and snapped open her small purse to pull out a lipgloss. "You asked."

Rounding on her, Olivia grabbed her arm. "You have done some crazy ass things before, Kate, but this…? And when did you have time to marry him? And to buy this?" She took a closer look at the ring on Kate's hand. "Wow! That's really—" Remembering herself, she shook her head and dropped the ring like the thing burned her.

"—pretty," Kate finished for her, staring down at the sparkly stone. "It's pretty and it's mine. At least temporarily, that is."

"What's that supposed to mean, *temporarily*? Nobody gets married temporarily."

"*We* did." Turning to the mirror, she glossed her lips with the peachy tint.

"Wh-what exactly are you saying? That you're not married for real?"

"Oh, we're married, all right, license and all. It's just…complicated. And I wasn't going to tell you. Or anyone."

"You weren't—? Kate, you were going to keep this from all of us? From your family who loves you? Is this about the stupid no-dating bet? Because if you impulsively married this guy just to get back at us—"

"No. It's not about that. I swear. But, just for the record, I didn't lose that bet."

"Oh, for the love of—! *Forget* the bet." Olivia started pacing again. "You need to tell me what's going on. I need the whole story. Beginning to end."

Kate sighed, knowing nothing else would do at this point. "Fine. But not right now. Tonight, I'm having dinner with Finn at a really, really nice restaurant that he went to a lot of trouble to get us into. So, you've got to promise not to tell anyone. It's our secret. Tell Jake not to say anything either." She took Olivia by the forearms. "Promise me."

"Okay. Fine. Tomorrow morning. Main Street Diner. Eight a.m. The truth and nothing but the truth."

Kate exhaled with a nod.

Olivia pulled her into a hug. "He seems like a nice guy and *gorgeous* and definitely an improvement over that—" she stopped herself—"over Cree Malone. So, I'll reserve judgment until after you tell me everything. And I won't say a word until then."

"Thanks, Liv." She should have known she could never keep a secret in a town as small as Marietta, or from Olivia, her best and oldest friend.

The old adage, "*No good deed goes unpunished*," came to mind. Just how much retribution would she be meted out for her decision to help Finn keep his children? Or for needing to put a period on an old paragraph of her life? Time would tell. Until then, all she could hope for was damage control.

THAT EVENING, WHEN they drove back to Marietta, he parked in front of her apartment and shut off the engine. For all intents and purposes, their lovely evening had ended with Olivia and Jake's unexpected appearance. What were the freaking odds they would show up at a restaurant so far out of town? He supposed that to expect the unexpected was becoming a way of life with him.

As much as he'd wanted Kate to come back with him tonight, to settle her into his home, she'd convinced him to wait until tomorrow, when the children would be up and they could introduce the idea of her-as-nanny together.

She was right, of course. But uneasiness tumbled through him at the idea that what they'd done today was as fragile as a bubble that might somehow burst by morning if they weren't together. But maybe that was just because he'd spent the last five years waiting for the other shoe to drop. Now that the shoe *had* dropped, with Melissa's custody grab, he could stop looking over his shoulder for impending doom. He could see the damn thing coming. But with Kate back in his life, he felt like he could breathe again for the first time in years.

Kate lingered in the passenger seat, gathering up her things. "I'm sorry about tonight," she said. "You went to a lot of trouble."

"None of that matters," he said. "As long as you don't change your mind."

A scowl furled her pale brow. "I wouldn't do that."

"Can't say that I'd blame you if you did. It's pretty off the hook, what we did today."

A soft smile curved her lips. "That's why it's perfect. As you said, anything less than crazy just wouldn't be enough."

He sighed and stared past her, toward her apartment. "My kids are already wild about you. You know that."

"I kinda like them, too." She brushed her fingers against the petals of the wilting Calla lilies, then seemed to realize what he was saying. "No, really. Don't worry about that, Finn. I promise I'll do everything in my power to protect them. Whatever issues we have, whatever stands between you and me, has nothing to do with your children. They're just kids. They had nothing to do with what happened in our past."

Her words made his chest constrict. What happened in their past did still stand between them. And maybe always would. She didn't trust him, and he supposed he deserved that. She'd claimed there might be a certain payback involved where Melissa was concerned, but he couldn't be sure whether she felt the same about him.

One thing he believed, however: she cared about his children. She might even come to love his children. But he would never have agreed to this if he didn't believe, with his whole heart, that Kate would never blame them for the mess he'd made of his and Kate's lives. Still, he was glad she'd said the words out loud. For him, this marriage might be a way to mend the past with Kate, but first, it was about keeping Cutter and Caylee.

The sun was down and the streetlights had come on in town. Marietta was mostly shut down by this hour and except for the crickets that chirped in the distance, the quiet seemed almost intimate as they got out and he walked her up the walkway to her door.

"What time should I come tomorrow?" she asked when they stopped on her stoop.

"Whenever you want. Or," he suggested, "come tonight." The invitation in that suggestion was just that—an invitation.

"No, tomorrow. I'll come over then." She reached into her purse searching for her keys.

He braced an arm on the door beside her head and leaned close. "So these rules of yours...specifically the one against kissing, don't technically, start until tomorrow, right?"

Her lips parted and she leaned back against the door. "Technically speaking, they're already in force."

"Yeah? Because I was thinking..." he said, softly, studying her eyes in the moonlight. They'd gone dark all of a sudden and she blinked up at him with the first hint of uncertainty he'd seen in her since they'd reconnected. He didn't touch her, but closed the distance between them until he was close enough to feel her heat. "Since I'm forced to leave you here at your own door on the night of our wedding, the least I can do is kiss you goodnight."

"That's...that's not a good idea."

It wasn't fear he saw in her eyes, but heat. Want. Maybe even need. Need he recognized from so long ago, when what was between them was a thing that made them both want to spend entire days in bed and made keeping their hands off each other nearly impossible. But that was then. He'd already stolen one kiss from her. The next one would have to be hers to steal.

"You're probably right," he conceded, dipping his face against her hair to catch the fragrance of her shampoo—

some lemony, minty thing that brought to mind long, cool drinks in the shade. Whether she meant to or not, she tilted her head back against the door as he brushed the tender skin of her neck with his lips. "Who knows what could happen, right? With a simple kiss between you and me?"

She swallowed thickly. "Right. I mean, it…wouldn't change anything, because—" Her words fell off then, as his tongue dampened a spot on her throat.

"Because?" he asked.

"—because abiding by the rules will protect us."

"From what?" he whispered, brushing his mouth up the side of her throat until he felt her quake. He heard her keys drop from her fingers and hit the concrete step. Her eyes flew open at the sound.

"From going where we both know we shouldn't go," she said, placing her hands against his chest and gently pushing him away.

He took a step back, reining in whatever had just been about to happen between them. He'd heard her rules and tonight was probably too soon to try to break them. But he damn well intended to break them.

Kate was like a concrete-coated flower whose outsides needed chipping away. That tough exterior was a façade that even she was convinced was real. The girl who didn't believe in love anymore, the one who dallied with tattooed musicians who wouldn't have the vaguest idea what to do with a woman like her, even if he could catch her, *that* Kate wasn't the same one he'd known back in Missoula. He guessed he was the one who'd put that coating there, and the one who'd have to chip the damned stuff away.

With a slow smile at the look on her face, he reached down and retrieved the keys for her. "Better get inside, you. I gotta get home to the kids. Past Izzy's bedtime."

Settling the keys into her palm, he backed away, then headed down the two steps to the sidewalk.

"Finn?" she called, still braced with her back to the door.

"Yeah?"

She thought better of whatever she'd been about to say and simply said, "See you tomorrow."

He nodded. "Night, Kate."

KATE AND OLIVIA met at the Main Street Diner the next morning, but the place was so crowded, they decided to duck into the less crowded Java Café and take a walk instead. Kate ordered coffee and two blueberry scones from Sally Driscoll, the barista, and handed one to her sister. Outside, they strolled past the quaint, red-brick western store fronts on Main Street, where banners decorated every lamp post, announcing the upcoming 77th Annual Copper Mountain Rodeo.

The rodeo itself had become the grand finale to a premier event in Marietta that few locals missed, complete with a grand dinner right here on Main Street and dancing in the park. A momentary weakness had her imagining dancing under the twinkling lights with Finn, letting him hold her close, pretending they really belonged together.

She pushed such insidious thoughts from her mind and refocused on the task at hand.

It took two long blocks, winding down Collier and Church Avenues, to explain her convoluted situation to Olivia. And even as she talked, she was still trying to sort the whole mess in her own mind. She'd barely slept at all last night, fretting about moving in today. Enlisting Olivia to keep her secret kind of paled in comparison to what the rest of the day might hold with Finn's children.

As they began the loop again, they passed Sage Carrigan's Copper Mountain Chocolate Shop, they stopped in unison and stared at the pretty goodies in the window like puppies eyeing cheese. Olivia took a sip of strong coffee, considering the madness of Kate's new 'arrangement.'

"Almost more shocking," she said at last, "than the fact that you married this guy to help him after what went down between you, is the fact that I never knew about any of it."

Her words broke the chocolate spell Kate had fallen under. There was hurt in Olivia's expression. She couldn't blame her. "I know, I know," Kate said with a guilty look at her sister. "I'm sorry."

Olivia paused with a sigh. "But why? Why would you keep it from us? Not let us help you through it?"

"I'm...I don't know, Liv. I think...initially, I was afraid

it wouldn't last. And then, that I would screw it up.

"I'm your sister. Okay, but…not about him, six years ago, or the other woman or, more importantly, the fact that you're still in love with him now."

"No, I'm not! Not even close. We're water under the bridge, Olivia. We happened a long time ago and now he's got these children and another whole life."

"A life that includes you."

"Just temporarily."

"And you expect to skip away from this whole affair scot-free? Pardon the pun. No harm, no foul? C'mon, Kate. What if you fall for the kids? What if you fall for him again, and he doesn't fall for you? What if he breaks your heart?"

"I don't fall, Olivia. Not anymore. And he can't break my heart twice. I won't let him. Clearly, he was just grasping at whatever female was near enough to keep his head above water with the court and his ex-wife. I'm just…convenient. But in his defense, I was the one who proposed marrying him this way. Not him." *Sort of.*

"Interesting. He didn't seem to be looking at you like you were just 'convenient' last night."

"What do you mean? How was he looking at me?" *Like he wanted to run when her family had shown up? Like he wished he could disappear?*

"Like he's crazy about you. You'd have to be a blind person not to see that in his eyes. Even Jake commented about it after we left. And he's a guy."

Had he been looking at her that way? No doubt he was simply flushed with embarrassment at having been caught at that restaurant by her family. Yes, he'd kissed her. But lusting and choosing were two different things. And they both knew, when push came to shove, whom he'd chosen and why.

"So you have no feelings toward him."

Feelings? Oh, she had plenty of those. Like feeling her legs go weak when he'd dragged his mouth up her throat last night at her door. Or the dumb, impossible feelings running through her as she watched him with his children—children that he'd had with Melissa.

And just thinking about him now made her nipples harden into tight little buds. But that didn't constitute…love. Love was that thing that bound two people together through thick and thin, and made a person recognize the right person when they were standing in front of them. A feat she'd been incapable of, even six years ago, when she'd suggested they take a break while she went abroad. That had been her fault. Sleeping with Melissa had been his.

"I might hate him. Or want him." She took her last bite of scone. "Or hate him."

Olivia tilted a headshake at her. "Oh, Katie…"

"But a long-term relationship? No. Falling in love is just not in my DNA anymore. I am, as you so rudely pointed out, a serial dater. I date frogs, flawed princes and drunken musicians. But potential husbands? No."

"Yeah," Olivia said, "Need I point out that you already have one of those *and* a ring?"

Kate brushed the crumbs from her hands and tossed the waxed paper bag into a nearby trash can. "Fake and flawed."

"Flaws come with the territory, babe. Men are flawed creatures. So are we, come to think of it."

"What about your Jake? He's gorgeous, successful and free of glow-in-the-dark skeletons in his closet."

Olivia smiled a little dreamily and sighed. "Well, Jake… He's the exception to every rule."

"Okay, now you're just making me nauseous."

Olivia giggled and took Kate's arm, walking toward the intersection of Main Street again. "You know I'm kidding, right? We both had our issues when we met up again. God knows, I did. And Jake has his stuff from his time in Afghanistan. It's getting better, but he still deals with it. And there's scaring the pants off me in that helicopter of his, as he defies gravity. And then, there's toothpaste cap thing…"

"You cannot equate toothpaste caps with pregnant buckle bunnies set on ruining your life."

"I know. There are problems and then there are problems," Olivia agreed. "Now Kyle, my ex, was a *Problem* with a capital *P*, which is now, thankfully, finally behind me. But whatever my or Jake's issues are, they're footnotes in a relationship that's overwhelmingly good. Yours and Finn's? What happened between you is like a rockslide that came out of nowhere, but maybe those rocks are not so insurmountable. Maybe they could build a bridge between you two."

"You're saying the children are rocks."

She shook her head. "The children are the bridge, *built* with the rocks."

Kate sniffed. "You're supposed to be the voice of reason here, dragging me back from the edge. Weren't you the one preaching relationship abstinence to me just last week?"

"I was saving you from certain ruin with Beelzebub Malone. I was not talking about a gorgeous, long-lost love who actually put a ring on it."

"This is not at all how I imagined this conversation going," Kate said. "Are you going to keep my secret or not?"

She considered. "Yes, because you need some time to sort things out. But eventually, you're going to have to tell Dad and Jaycee. You and I just walked the entire bounds of Marietta. In other words, cough and someone will hear you. Your secret is bound to get out. But what's done is done. You married him. You agreed to help him. Maybe this was all just Fate's way of intervening. *Maybe*," she suggested, leaning in close for the whisper, "you two are really perfect for each other."

Chapter Six

FINN AND THE twins had the morning set aside to work on the tree house they'd been designing for weeks. Cutter and Caylee had given him a few dozen crayon pictures of what they wanted and he, in turn, had turned those drawings into real designs until they'd all agreed. Carpentry was a secret hobby of his, something he'd learned at the side of a next-door neighbor, growing up.

Tom Landin was an unmarried, string-bean of a career carpenter who'd probably felt sorry for the boy growing up next door without a father. For reasons Finn could hardly fathom until much later in life, Landin had made a point of inviting that lonely boy to join him on Saturday projects at his house to learn how to handle wood. Thinking of him now, he could still remember the sweet scent of pipe smoke and the tang of freshly cut wood-shavings that clung to him like a spring rain and the easy smile that nearly always lingered on his lips as he hummed some tuneless song while he worked.

Mr. Landin had fondly called him Huckleberry and, together, they'd built everything from fences to rabbit cages to treasure chests.

His favorite project, by far, was the simple treehouse Tom had helped him construct in the woods near their mobile home, which he and a group of friends christened as their clubhouse several years later. But none of those days spent high in that old tree meant more to him than the time Mr. Landin had spent building the treehouse with him. Time he'd given freely to him for no other reason than to fill that vacancy in a lonely boy's life. He'd been a surrogate father to him for many critical, lonely years before passing suddenly of a heart attack one ordinary Friday night, when the world wasn't watching and Finn had been busy with other, teenaged things.

Nothing—until the loss of Kate six years ago—had ever hit him as hard. He'd worked most of the summer to build the miniature facsimile of the treehouse Mr. Landin had built for him, which he'd placed beside his grave in the crook of an overhanging tree. In the years since, no one had touched the model that still stood, watching over that solitary plot in the ocean of unadorned headstones in that Helena cemetery.

He shook off the thought, watching his own children sort through the stack of wood he'd had delivered from the mill as he measured and cut it. If he could leave his children with memories half as rich as the ones he had of his old friend, then he'd know he'd done something right.

His throat felt thick as he watched them crawl around the pile of lumber, finding the right pieces and delivering them to his table saw. They were growing so fast. Seemed like just yesterday they were bawling babies that needed everything he had to give. Now, they were independent little souls who conspired and found their own trouble together, but still, thank God, loved a good story at bedtime. Still came to him for a Band-Aid and a hug.

He looked away, in an attempt to contain the inevitable emotions that rose at the thought of losing them, even part-time. Melissa had no idea who these children were and he doubted she'd have any clue what to do with them if she won them. Certainly they had no idea who she was.

Wrestling with the decision to tell them or not to tell them still kept him up at night. Was it fair, if she managed to win, to spring such an earthquake on them suddenly? Fair to worry them needlessly if she lost? He hoped somehow, the answers to those questions would become clearer in the weeks to come.

Just like he hoped he'd get clear about Kate.

As if he'd conjured her with his thoughts, he turned to find her standing at the side of his house holding a pink box tied with a string. She smiled as the children abandoned the lumber pile and ran up to her. She gathered them up in a hug and reached out to fluff their hair.

He felt his stomach drop at the sight of her, all wind-blown and beautiful from the car ride out here. She had on bling-y sandals, one of those long, flowy skirts and a silky tank the color of sunshine.

The fire he kept banked inside him flared like an oxygen-fed flame as he walked toward her. "Hey," he said, smiling and stopping a few feet from her. He dropped his hands on Caylee's shoulders.

"Hey," she replied a little breathlessly, her nerves showing. "What are you building over there?"

"Our treehouse! You want to help?" Cutter said, waving his casted green arm.

She laughed. "A *treehouse*? You lucky ducks. Do I want to help? Are you kidding? Of course! I just didn't know your daddy was so handy." She gave him a look that stirred up all kinds of handy thoughts.

"A man has to have a few secrets," he said. "What's in the box?"

"Yeah, what's in the box?" Caylee begged.

She lifted the pink container with a smile. "My own secret...that I will share once we all find a seat on the grass."

The twins laughed then raced each other back to the tree-shaded patch of grass.

"Once a kindergarten teacher..." he teased.

"That's right." She handed him the box. "Never let it be said that bribes and five-year-olds don't mix. You couldn't very well christen your new house without cupcakes. Consider them my version of a salt and bread housewarming gift with a little bribe on the side."

"All cupcakes and graft are welcome." They turned to follow the children back to the cool shade of the three-trunked cottonwood. Finn untied the box and peeked inside. "Who wants dessert for lunch?"

The cupcakes in the bakery box were chocolate with frosting ladybugs decorating the top and the four of them settled onto the grass to partake.

"So," he began, as the children licked the chocolate from their lips. "Miss Canaday is going to be staying with us awhile. She's going to be your new nanny."

Cutter tucked his chin in, in that cute, wide-eyed way he had. "What's a *nanny?*"

"That's a fancy way of saying 'babysitter,'" Kate explained. "I'll be taking care of you while your dad works hard on your new ranch."

"But you're a teacher," Caylee pointed out. Always the practical one.

"True, I am. But the regular teacher in my class, the one I was helping, is coming back early. So for now, I'm just going to take care of you." Those simple words, coming from her own lips, resonated in a new way, despite the fact that she'd practiced them over and over before coming. To say them to these two little human beings, whose hearts were so visible in their wide eyes, made the whole thing suddenly real.

"For a while?" Cutter asked, suddenly anxious. "But how long?"

Kate's eyes flicked to his. He addressed his answer to her with a questioning lift of his brow. "Umm…well, let's not worry about that just yet," she said.

The boy's troubled gaze fell to the blades of grass that poked his bare calves and he ripped out a handful, spreading them in his chubby palm. "Did you know birds make their nests out of dried grass?" He held the sprinkle of grass out to show her.

"They do?"

He nodded. "They weave the grass together and glue it with mud. So the babies don't fall out and get lost. There's one in this tree. See it?" He pointed to a branch up high.

The September leaves still clung stubbornly to the branches and she couldn't spot the thing, but she pretended to as he spilled the grass into her hand. "We'll have to keep an eye out to see what kind of bird made it."

"Okay." Cutter jumped up and turned to the wood pile. "Are we gonna build the treehouse or what?"

"What about Izzy?" Caylee asked, unpeeling the last of the paper sleeve from her cupcake with deliberate care.

"You know Izzy," he said, "she's really busy with school right now. Don't worry. We'll still see her sometimes. Maybe when Daddy and Miss Canaday want to go out to dinner."

"On a *date*?" Caylee—whose mind was no longer on the source of her soon-to-come sugar rush, but now wholly on Kate—eyed her with a spaniel-like head tilt.

"What? No! *Not* on a date." Kate simultaneously laughed

and shot Finn the evil eye. "We're not dating. I'm just your nanny."

Caylee, female to the core, reserved judgment with an assessing glance between the two adults. "But you can if you *want* to," she said, with a coy smile, then jumped up to join her brother.

Kate exhaled a breath she hadn't realized she was holding. Leave it to a five-year-old to strike at the heart of the matter.

"That went well," he said to her when his daughter was out of earshot.

"Did it?"

"You won them over with the cupcakes." He grinned at her with a look that she felt all the way to her toes, then told the twins, "Let's help Miss Canaday get her things out of the car before we get back to the treehouse. Who wants to show her where her room is?"

AT THE END that long, first day of treehouse building, barbequing and dancing around the realities of Kate's arrival, Finn read stories to the twins and kissed them goodnight. A glance around this room, though, reminded him that their room needed a fresh coat of paint, as practically every other room in the house did. All he needed was a few dozen more hours in his day.

By the time he flipped off the light switch, Cutter was

already asleep, but Caylee sat up in the dark. "Daddy?" she whispered.

He moved back to her bed and sat down. "What is it, darlin'?"

"Do you like Miss Candy?"

"Sure I do. Very much. Or I wouldn't have asked her to… to be your nanny."

"No, I mean, do you *like* her?"

It was a grown-up kind of question for this child to be asking. Inside that, was the longing he often saw in her eyes for a woman in her life. A mother. She was just getting to the age where she'd begun to realize that not all families had only daddies. The question stabbed at him, because what she was really asking was, "Is it *her*?"

"Sure, I like her. But we're just friends," he lied, sticking to the script that would be the easiest for them to swallow. The one that would cause them the least amount of heartbreak.

"Oh." Caylee spun a strand of hair around her finger, brushing the lock against her cheek, her lifelong way of comforting herself. "Like Izzy?"

"Not exactly like Izzy, no," he admitted, brushing a kiss on the child's forehead. "Izzy is very young. Miss Candy is…"

"Pretty?" she finished.

He grinned, recalling Kate's playful smile as she handed up the lumber to him in the tree today. "Yeah, she *is* pretty, isn't she?"

"I wish…" Caylee began, then called back her words. "Never mind."

"What do you wish?"

"Nothing. Night, Daddy."

"G'night, you. See you later, alligator."

Caylee yawned. "In a while, crocodile."

Kate was outside on the covered porch when he found her sitting on the rickety porch swing that had probably been hanging there for twenty years. She had a beer in her hand and another one already cracked open for him.

"I thought you could use one of these after today," she told him. "I know I can."

He took the beer and tested the chain with a little tug before sinking down beside her. The swing creaked as sat and he stared out at the land that had so recently become his. The early September moon was rising against a darkening, deep blue sky. In the distance, the shadowy Absarokas blotted out the bottom half of the sky where they fingered up from the horizon. Stars were beginning to twinkle and bats had come out to play.

He took a gulp of beer, still shaken by Caylee's questions.

"You look exhausted," Kate said.

He sighed. "You, too."

"Your kids…" she said, tilting a smile at him, "they're great. And it's been all you. You have done an amazing job with them."

It might have been the first time someone had actually said that to him. The words meant even more, coming from her. "This is only your first day," he warned. "You may be begging for mercy before long."

She nodded. "Single parenting is not for wimps." After she said it, she glanced at him quickly. "I-I mean—"

"I know what you meant. And you're right. Kinda felt nice today, sharing the job." Before she could remind him of the temporary nature of her position, he pointed up at a shooting star, trailing across the darkening sky. "Ahh, did you see that?"

Kate followed his finger with her gaze and shook her head. "I missed it."

"Keep watching. There'll be another along soon. This is the season for them."

And though she kept her eyes on the star-smattered sky, the twinkling lights denied her. The evening had cooled off the heat of the day and that sweet Montana smell perfumed the air.

"You never told me you were a carpenter," she said, turning to him. "That treehouse is going to be amazing. I wish I'd had one like that. But my father was a lawyer, not a treehouse builder."

He grinned and took another sip of beer. "And I'm a bull rider, not a lawyer...a skill I wish I had right now."

"You're going to win, Finn."

He shrugged. "You learn fortune telling since we saw each other last?"

She made a face. "Women's intuition?"

With a nod, he leaned against the wooden back of the benched swing. "What does that intuition tell you about us?"

She slid a look at him. "Us?"

"Yeah. You and me. The bull-riding rancher and the nanny."

"Maybe that beer was a bad idea."

"No. It's a simple question, Kate."

Staring back out over his pasture she said, "You know the ground rules. Don't try to change them now."

"You can't still hate me. At least, it sure didn't feel that way when I kissed you."

She sighed. "Do I seem the same to you, Finn? As the girl you gave that ring to six years ago?"

He frowned. "The same? No, but then, neither am I. That doesn't mean—"

"Because I'm not. I'm not that girl at all anymore. I agreed to help you because of what we had once. Because you needed help. Because, okay, I don't hate you. And I would help any old friend who needed my help. But I don't do 'relationships' anymore. I'm not a long-term kinda girl. Maybe I never was." She stared down at the long neck of her beer bottle and rubbed her thumb across the top. "I probably would have screwed everything up anyway. Probably the smartest thing you ever did was walk away from me."

A creaking sound from somewhere above them drew their gazes and a moment later, Kate shrieked as the porch swing ripped from its moorings and crashed to the porch floor. The two of them sprawled together in the broken remains of the swing, with Kate half-lying atop him. Laughter bubbled up between them as she tried to crawl off his chest.

He stopped her with a hand and tugged her closer. "You okay?"

She nodded with another laugh and held up her beer. "She falls! She recovers! You?"

His was still safe in his hand as well. "Yup." Brushing the hair off her face, he glanced at the wreckage around him and said, "Well, I guess I'll have to fix that, too."

Her heart thudded against the wall his chest, her fingers curled in the fabric of his shirt. He went instantly hard as her gaze settled on his mouth for a long consideration before those green eyes of hers lifted to his with something like...apology or regret. He moved his head fractionally toward her, to which she leaned an equal distance back.

"Lemme ask you a question," he said softly, relenting. "You more afraid that you can't fall in love with me again, or that you might?"

She exhaled a breath. "I'm not afraid at all, in case you hadn't noticed. Maybe it's you who should be."

She pushed off his chest and got to her feet. "G'night."

"Night." As she disappeared into the house, he took a

long swig of beer, laid his head back amidst the ruins of the swing, and watched another dying star shoot across the sky.

THEIR FIRST WEEK passed by in a blur, with the kids going back and forth to school, Finn disappearing for most of the day, fixing broken fences, with new posts and barbed wire, all of which left Kate feeling at loose ends and alone in his house.

She and lonely loose ends were not friends. So instead of her kneejerk solution to this problem—namely finding a short term man to fill a long term problem—she looked around Finn's new home for something to keep her busy.

Though he had never been one to complain about gift horses, the ranch house he'd inherited was a monument to the seventies, with tile countertops in the kitchen and funky paint on every wall. The bad shag carpeting harbored God knew what and the bathtubs had rust stains. Nothing that a little elbow grease, paint and a few extra dollars wouldn't fix.

What this place didn't feel like was a home for Finn and the twins. Not with boxes still stacked, unpacked, in nearly every corner and the twins sleeping in a room that had green shag carpeting and dark blue walls that worked on her gag reflex.

Kate figured that while the kids were in school and Finn was in the fields, in the time she had here, at least she could make a dent in some of what needed to be done.

She tackled the boxes first and emptied them to the best of her ability, finding places for most everything.

A prowl through the garage the next day turned up the paint and supplies he had already purchased to paint every wall in the house. Every gallon white.

Typical man.

So she drove a couple of gallons to the Big Z Hardware store in town and had Paul Zabrinski mix up some color into them.

Her stepmother, Jaycee, had been the painter in their family and practically a pro. *When you have to depend solely on yourself to get things done,* she'd told them early, *you figure out a way.* So she'd put a paintbrush in all three sisters' hands and taught them how to paint walls.

That day Kate had ripped out the nasty carpeting in the twins' room and found beautiful hardwood floors below. Then the next day, she primed and washed the bedroom walls and ceiling with a soft blue and trimmed the room in a creamy white. Just that much utterly transformed the room. But she had other ideas, as well.

She slid the twins' mattresses on the floor in her room for the night and locked away the surprise of their room until she was finished.

From the sidelines, Finn watched quietly and said nothing about her efforts, except to wonder with his children what she was up to in there. He seemed to have taken her words to heart the other night and deliberately kept his distance. When he wasn't working, putting the ramshackle ranch back together, he was spending time with the twins, even working after dinner on the treehouse until the moon began to rise and bedtime arrived. Soon after, he would disappear into his own room as well. And the next day, the dance would all begin again.

When their paths crossed, longing would blindside her. Often, that kiss they'd shared at his door that night, or the one at the courthouse, would come flooding back. And dampness would spread between her legs, as she imagined the slide of his tongue against hers, or the smooth curve of his muscled arms beneath her hands.

At night, she'd lie, exhausted, in her lonely bed and stare at the ceiling, wondering what, exactly, she'd managed to get herself into? Was he already regretting their arrangement? Had she been wrong to push him away?

No. Staying apart was in both of their best interests, but having him *actually* distance himself from her stung more than she could have imagined. She'd meant it, hadn't she? All of her rules? While her head said, "Yes!" every other part of her sighed, "Let me think about this again."

Then, something out of the blue would happen, like the morning she checked her email and found a serious teaching job offer from a school up in Missoula, starting October fifth. The job was for the rest of the school year and possibly, a continuing contract for the next year. The position wasn't even one she'd applied for, but, according to the email, the principal of that school was friends with Judy Elsworth, the principal of Marietta Elementary, where Kate had worked for the last two years and who'd recommended Kate for the job.

Missoula. October fifth. Less than a month away and two hundred and something miles away from here. Still, she reasoned, *after* Finn's court date. The opportunity couldn't be more timely.

But the email caused her to begin to hyperventilate and she quickly shut her laptop. They needed an answer within the week and she felt incapable of responding right then. She'd only just gotten here and already, she was planning her exit strategy? Of course she was. That was her M.O., wasn't it?

Sitting alone in Finn's kitchen, Kate closed her eyes and decided to wait to answer that email. No rush. She had time.

But she walked over to a kitchen drawer, took out one of the twins' brown paper lunch sacks and cupped it around her mouth, breathing in and slowly out, until she stopped feeling dizzy—telling herself she'd think about Missoula later.

After putting the finishing touches on the room on the fourth day, she decided to wait until nighttime to reveal it. So, she managed to keep the children occupied, helping with dinner chores. Both were hungry for time spent with Kate and working together in the kitchen was a glorious mess.

Kate chopped up strawberries and let Caylee stir them into a bowl of whipped cream, as Cutter pilfered pieces of the graham cracker crust he'd helped make for a special pie.

"Why don't you have any children, Miss Candy?" Caylee asked Kate as she stirred.

The question caught her off guard. *Almost thirty and still on my own.* That certainly didn't fit the picture she'd had for herself ten years ago. Or even six. Once, she'd imagined a big family for herself, but that dream had, somehow, faded away with the disappearance of that other girl she used to be.

How the hell had she allowed things to go so awry? She'd hardly noticed it, in fact, until Eve and Olivia smacked her down for it. Perhaps that wasn't precisely true. Perhaps denying that person she'd become was easier if she didn't look too closely.

"Nope, no children," she told Caylee. "And why don't we dispense with the 'Miss Candy' thing. You can just call me Kate. All right?"

"Kate," Cutter said, without missing a beat while licking whipped cream off his entire palm, "have you ever been to the rodeo?"

"I have. Have you?"

"No, but Daddy rides in the rodeo sometimes. He says maybe he'll let us come sometime, but he never does. Do you think you can make him bring us next time?"

"Well, now. That's up to your dad. But I can put in a good word with him for you."

"Put in a good word with who?" Finn's voice came from behind her as he walked in the door.

He looked exhausted, wearing half the dust from the pasture on him and, as he hung his hat on the old peg near the door, he took in the little scene in his kitchen with a look she couldn't begin to decipher.

"Well, with you, of course," Kate answered. "Cutter was just asking if he could come along to watch one of your rodeos sometime." She lifted her eyebrows at him with a secret signal. "I said I'd ask you."

"Snip, you don't need to go through Miss Canaday. You can come to me direct."

"I already did," he whined, "and you said—"

"Soon. That's what I said." He moved to the sink to wash his hands and splash water on his face.

Cutter grumbled to himself. "And she told us to say Kate. Not Miss Candy."

Finn slid a look at Kate, who affirmed Cutter's words.

"Is everything okay?" she asked, moving up beside him.

He braced his hands on the sink and hung his head down wearily between them. "You mean besides the pond needing a good dredge, the automatic pellet feeder being rusted through in two places and the hay barn needing a new roof and, oh, yeah. A roofer? Yeah. Everything's great." He ran his damp hands through his hair and made a stab at starting over. "Sorry. None of that's your problem."

"Doesn't mean I don't care."

His hazel eyes met hers and softened. "I'll manage." The delicious scent of her gooey homemade lasagna wafted from the oven. "Something smells good."

"We both helped. And we made a pie!" Caylee said proudly.

For the first time since he'd walked in the door, Finn smiled. "Well, that looks good enough to eat. Is it all for me? Or do I have to share?"

"Ohhh, Daddy. We all get some."

"The pie needs to chill awhile." Relieved to see the tension broken, Kate stuck the pie in the fridge and pulled the lasagna out of the oven. "First we eat dinner."

"Then we see the surprise!" Cutter said.

Finn stared over the heads of his children at Kate in a way that made her flutter inside. Was it because of the snapshot of domesticity that she and his children made in his kitchen? Or was it because, maybe for the first time in their short lives, they were doing the things other children simply took for granted? She couldn't deny she had enjoyed herself immensely these past few days, too, or that working on the house had not been a chore, but a secret joy.

Now, after a day of allowing herself to almost forget who she was and what they were doing, alarm bells went off in her head at his look, warning her of getting too comfortable with all this. This wasn't her life, her home, or even her man. She was a substitute for the real thing. A temporary substitute. As long as she remembered that, they would all be fine.

"CLOSE YOUR EYES," Kate told the children, later, as they

stood outside their bedroom door. "No peeking."

Finn felt a prickle of anticipation rush across him at the excitement in his children's eyes. She'd been working on something in secret all week. It had been a long time since he'd seen them this happy, as if this was Christmas morning. Kate, herself, looked like the cat who'd gotten into the cream as she guided the kids into the freshly painted room. When they opened their eyes, they both squealed.

He had to admit, she'd worked a mini-miracle with the room, turning the ceiling into a piece of Montana sky with washes of white clouds spilling across the ceiling and down the walls. She'd even repainted the old chest that stood in the center of one wall and put coordinating coverlets and throw pillows on each of their beds and a striped throw rug on the floor between.

The twins raced to their beds and flopped down to stare up at their painted sky.

He was staring, not at the room, but at her.

"Wait for it," she told them, then flipped the light switch. Glow in the dark stars lit the darkened ceiling like the Milky Way and a three dimensional moon glowed over the closet door.

Cutter was laughing and Caylee couldn't stop staring with a silly smile on her face.

"Look at the Big Dropper!" Cutter said to Caylee.

"That's 'Dipper,' Snip and what do you say to Miss—to Kate?" Finn said, still not taking his eyes off her. He watched a flush of color creep to her cheeks, and she kept her gaze on the kids, as if she feared in meeting his eye, she might reveal something she had no intention of revealing.

They rushed over to give her a hug and thank her. In the years since the birth of his twins, he'd learned about the pure generosity of children with their affections. His children's anyway. They did not edit, complicate or hold back their feelings. You always knew exactly where you stood. The good news was—they liked Kate. The bad news? They liked her a lot.

He'd tried like hell to keep his distance from her this week. Kept himself too busy to think about her. That had been the plan at least. Failed miserably. The harder he pushed back, the worse he felt.

After putting the kids to bed, he took a quick shower, then walked outside to look for her. The squeaky spring on the screen door gave him away. He spotted her sitting up in his half-built treehouse, sipping wine as the fireflies began to light up the night sky, and staring at the crazy swarm of stars that illuminated the black dome. The sight took his breath away for a moment—Kate bathed in starlight, smiling down at him.

Chapter Seven

"COULD THERE BE a more perfect place to look at the stars?" she asked, as he walked toward her perch. She patted the freshly cut wood. "I have wine and I'll share. Join me?"

Something tightened inside him at the thought. Hell yes, he would.

He climbed the makeshift ladder he'd nailed into the tree and she made room for him as he sat down beside her. The treehouse still lacked a roof and was basically only a platform and two walls. But directly above the platform was an opening in the tree, a view unfettered by branches where he planned to put a skylight for this very purpose when all was said and done.

There was nothing like a night sky in Montana. Nothing that could compare to how small that huge black, star-scattered expanse made one feel. Sitting out here at night seemed to put everything in perspective. His perspective felt a little at odd angles at the moment. He thought of the twins staring up at the miniature version she'd designed on their ceiling as they drifted off tonight, happy as puppies in grass.

"They asleep?" she asked.

"Like someone turned off a switch. Hey…thank you," he said simply.

She glanced back at him again, flashing a grin that stirred him up inside. He'd spent a good part of the last week trying to put that smile out of his mind, but he'd be damned if he'd managed to do it. And now, that smile made him want to drag her up against him and kiss her until she relinquished that misplaced control of hers. But, he did none of those things. Instead he sat beside her under the moonlight and coached himself in restraint.

"It was just a little whipped cream and strawberries," she said.

He chuckled and took a sip of wine straight from the bottle. "Yeah, thanks for the pie, too. But especially for the room. That was a lot of work that doesn't, in any way, fall under the nanny job description."

"My job description here is fuzzy at best, but you should know by now I pay no attention to the fine print." She reached for her neck and rubbed it. "And yeah, those little bitty stars nearly had me calling '*Uncle*,' but fixing that room was for fun and for free. Besides, I need to keep busy or I get a little stir-crazy."

He moved her hand aside and took over the neck rub for her. For a moment she stiffened, but then turned her back to give him access. As his hands dug into the knotted flesh of her shoulders and neck, he felt her relax.

"Ohhhh," she moaned. "*That…*that is…*thank you.*"

My pleasure. "You're welcome."

"I should be giving you the neck rub after the day you had. I'm sorry it's not going well."

The repairs around the ranch were sucking more dollars than he'd expected. His money issues simply meant he'd need to win a few more rodeos to get the stake he needed for that bull he wanted. But he could do that. Hell, yes, he could. "It'll be all right. I'll figure things out."

"I know." She dropped her head to give him better access. His fingers encountered the chain around her neck and as he went to lift it out of his way, he found her wedding and engagement rings dangling from the other end. She clapped her fingers around them as if to hide the rings, but, too late.

"At least you're wearing them," he said softly. When she said nothing in reply, to either acknowledge or deny that, he let them go, and dug his thumbs into the spot on her neck he remembered from when they were together before, the place where all of her tension gathered. There the knots still were, waiting for his fingers to find them.

Her skin was warm and silky soft. This close, he caught the scent of lavender in her hair and that female scent that belonged to her alone. There was something about Kate's scent that drove him crazy. Whatever else had changed, that remained constant.

A moment later, as his hands strayed to her upper arms,

she reached up to stay his fingers with her own and turned back to him. She studied him for a moment before she ended the contact between them. "Thanks. You always did have great hands." She stretched out on her back to stare upward. "C'mon. I was just about to search the sky for the meaning of life."

Fireflies winked in the darkness as he stretched out beside her and tucked his palms under his head, staring up at the sky. Overhead, they heard the swish and flap of bats' wings as the night creatures chased the flickering bugs. The purr of evening surrounded them. They lay like that for a long while, just staring at the stars, and again, tonight, shooting stars eluded them.

"Anything?" he finally asked.

"Nope. I got nothing."

"Me either."

She grinned and rolled a look at him. "Hey…about the rodeo and Cutter. You know I wasn't trying to get in the middle."

"I know. I wasn't upset with you. It was everything else. And he's right. I have been promising him." He sighed. "But so far, the rodeo is just a story he's heard me tell. The real thing can be a lot scarier for a five-year-old who's watching his dad possibly getting the shit kicked out of him under a bull."

With a worried look, Kate picked up a fistful of sawdust and tossed it over her left shoulder. "Pretend that was salt and bite your tongue. Besides," she added, "you can't really avoid taking him forever. It's what you do."

"Did," he corrected. "I'm only back at riding now for this place. And when I earn enough to keep us up and running, I'll give the rodeo up again."

"You know, you used to love bull riding."

A sigh escaped him. "I still do. In fact, if you don't love the rush of it, you've got no business on the back of a bull. But I'm not a kid anymore, and I can't afford to get hurt. Especially now, with this place. Which is why, if things work out with the PBR event in Springfield, Missouri this weekend, I plan on the Copper Mountain Rodeo being my last."

They'd discussed the Springfield event and Kate had agreed to watch the kids by herself for the few days he was gone. He'd be riding in a Pro Bull Riders Association rodeo and the prize money was too good to pass up. She wished he'd invited them all along, but she understood his need to protect the twins and decided not to take it personally.

He picked up a piece of scrap wood and ran his fingers along the edge of it. "I've been saving up for the last six years for a chance like this." He gestured to the fields around them. "This place fell in my lap because of Frank Greevy's generosity and, believe me, I'm grateful. But he was sick a long time and nothing's been touched here for years. The repairs on this place will take everything I have if I'm not careful, before I can even make it a working ranch. So the rodeo, it is."

She rolled toward him and braced her head on her hand. But she said nothing, just stared through the darkness at him.

"What?" he asked.

"I used to love watching you ride. Well, technically, I was scared to death watching you ride. But you could ride those bulls like nobody's business."

A pleased smile lifted one corner of his mouth. "Yeah?"

"Yeah. I don't think you should let anything keep you from doing the thing you love."

He rolled a look up at the stars. "My kids have put a whole different spin on my priorities."

She dropped her hand to the wooden floor between them and drew little circles in the dusty plank. "I know. I admire that about you. Mostly because I'm so *not* a grown up. At least, ask my family and they'll tell you that. My *many* choices in men have been…well, let's say flawed."

He squinted at her in the dark, a funny look that made her ask, "What? Do you want to know how many?"

"How many what?"

"Men. How many men there have been?"

"No. I wasn't going to ask that."

"What *were* you going to ask?"

"I was wondering how they didn't see in you what I do. How they let you go."

Oh, no. No, no, no. Don't say things like that to me.

He touched the diamond rings that dangled against her

blouse.

She laughed and pulled the rings back. "I just have them there for safe-keeping. Don't go getting any ideas."

He rolled up on his elbow toward her now with a grin. "Like…what kind of ideas?"

"Like…like…that this means something."

"Does it?"

She clutched the rings between her fingers like a nervous habit. "No."

But even in the moonlight, under those stars, he could see the lie in her eyes. She could have kept them in a drawer, out of sight. But she hadn't. They were nestled against her breasts, the precious metal warm from her skin.

Maybe the starlight was to blame, or the fact that they were up here in this treehouse when they should be doing the right thing, but he didn't feel like doing the right thing. He didn't feel like doing anything at the moment but what was wrong. She gasped as he slid his hand around her waist and pulled her close to him. "Maybe I don't believe you," he whispered against her mouth.

She swallowed thickly and flattened her palm against his chest. "You're playing with fire."

"Maybe I like it." He tucked her against his hips, just so there'd be no mistaking just how hot that fire really was. A tremor of want went through her and her fingers curled into his shirt. "And maybe you do, too."

"I *don't*."

"Prove it. I dare you." His mouth hovered teasingly close, his lips barely brushing hers.

"*Gawd*," she breathed against his mouth with a smile he could feel. "What's the deal with everyone *daring* me lately?"

But then she kissed him, and it was no gentle thing. Her kiss was hungry and full of hot need. She opened to him, wanting his tongue, finding his with hers until they couldn't get any closer. Until that kiss fused them together. He felt her arms tangle around his neck, restless and tugging him closer yet.

Damn, she tasted good. Red wine and sweet strawberries. And Kate.

An instant later she was on her back and he was on top of her, pushing his knee between her long legs and reveling in the soft press of her breasts against the hard plane of his chest. But he wanted—needed—her closer yet. He wanted inside her. Not just physically, but past that steely wall she'd closed around herself. He wanted all of her, not just the piece she'd agreed to loan him.

He slid his hands up her wrists and pinned them beside her head as he dropped a kiss against her ear, her neck, the little notch in her collarbone. Her hips shifted underneath him, tilting against his aching erection. He answered her movement in kind and she curled her leg around the back of his with a mewl of need.

Tugging the silky tank down the front of her breasts, he left a damp trail of kisses down to her lacy bra, which he pushed aside as well. And when his mouth closed over that tight little bud and he gave a little tug, she arched upward with a little gasp of pleasure.

"Ohhhh…" Her fingers twined with his. "This proves…nothing."

"I disagree," he murmured against the silky, soft skin of her breast.

"Okay," she breathed, "It proves I…I have no willpower. Under the stars…in a treehouse."

A grin tugged at his mouth as he released her hands and trailed one of his downward, along the curve of her breast and farther down. "Duly noted." He tugged up the hem of her long skirt, sliding his palm along her smooth, toned legs and tried to recall how many times he'd dreamed of doing just this in the last six years.

She settled her hands on his shoulders, rocking her head back and forth. "No, really, Finn. We shouldn't. This is…this is all wrong."

"You want me to stop?" He let go of her hand and pushed aside the hem of her skirt until his hand cupped her at the damp juncture of her legs. Languidly, he touched her there through her panties. "Ah, God, you're so wet. I don't think you do." She sucked in a breath and dropped her fingers into his hair with a slow tug. And just that made him come close to losing it. He clenched his jaw and slammed his eyes shut. "But I'll stop if you tell me to."

"But…but the rules—"

"Screw the rules. You made 'em. You can break 'em."

Kate knew very well that he was right. But she punished him for that suggestion with a little nip at his throat with her teeth, which she followed with a kiss. She felt a quake rock through him which only aggravated her need for more of the same.

She thought she'd prepared herself for a scenario like this. She'd imagined all the arguments pro and con and argued them all in her mind a dozen times. But once he touched her, logic and common sense abandoned her like a flock of birds at the crack of a gun. She felt adrift on his touch. Hungry for more. And as lost as she'd ever felt in her life.

"You think we'll come out of this unscathed," she murmured, catching his hand before he could dip his fingers into her heat. "But we won't. We can't undo this."

"I don't want to undo it—" And to prove his point, he tugged her panties aside and slid a finger into her. Lifting his head, he watched her arguments collapse and her eyes slide shut. He always had known just where to touch her to make her lose her mind. "Do *you*?"

She gasped. "That's…so unfair of you to ask me…now, when you're…"

"When I'm…?"

"Doing *that*."

"Who said anything about fair?"

Ahhh! Nobody.

He added another finger to the mix, slipping in and out of her with a maddening slowness until she was shaking with need. Her breath was a wild thing, trapped in her throat and all she could think was: *please don't stop*. Who cared about silly rules when he was...*ohhhh!* Her back arched and she bent her knees, welcoming him into the valley of her hips in reckless abandon. Vaguely, in some prehistoric part of her brain, that recklessness triggered a warning light. But that light was dim and blinking.

Dipping his mouth to her nipple again, he teased the nub with his tongue and sucked her hard. "You taste so damned good," he breathed against her skin.

She gasped, sliding her own hand down between them to feel his hard length against her palm. One by one, her arguments 'against' doing what they both seemed to want chipped and fell away. And all the arguments 'for,' waved little flags, shouting "*What's your problem?*"

Her fingers tugged at the button on his jeans. "I want—" she began, but he claimed her mouth again with a groan of pleasure. He pushed himself up on one hand and flicked open the buttons on his jeans, one-handed. She slid her hand up the hard contours of his arm, a touch that churned her thoughts and made her lose her place. What had she been about to say?

Oh, yes. Now she recalled.

"Okay," she whispered. "I have nothing to prove." She shoved the waistband of his jeans past his hipbones but he stopped her hand. "Please, Finn…"

"You're so sweet and wet. But we'll have to continue this inside. I didn't bring protection," he nearly growled.

She tilted her hips against his hand and blurted, "I'm on the *pill*—" before she could stop herself.

She heard him swallow thickly as his hips ground against her hips in an ancient motion, as his hand did miraculous things. "You sure?"

"Yes! I'm positive!"

"I mean about this."

Oh. "Stop talking or I'll lose my nerve."

And his fingers found that very nerve she mentioned. She squirmed against him. It had been a long, long time since anyone had touched her this way, or even cared enough to touch her this way. For a moment, she allowed herself to forget her resolve.

With one finger, he tugged down the silky panties that stood in his way and poised himself at the apex of her legs. He stared down at her in the darkness, his eyes on hers, saying something she couldn't make out. Something intentional and deeper than this moment or anything he was about to give her.

And then he slid inside her, filling her, and she nearly cried out with pleasure. His hard velvet stroked her, slowly at first, drawing her ever toward that unfathomable edge that made her thrash her head side to side and moan out loud. "Oh, you feel so good!"

The thrust of his hips seemed to accelerate at her words, moving faster of their own accord, until he seemed to lose control altogether and curve down around her to take all of her into his arms. Grinding, grinding, the friction between them grew unbearable until she tightened around him, spinning off out of control and flying apart. And when she did, he took his own, pounding into her until she felt him come hard and fast inside her. And with her arms and legs wrapped around him in the dark, up high in the tree, she welcomed him and everything he had to give.

THEY LAY, SPENT and sated under the stars on the hard planked floor of the treehouse for a long time afterward. Neither of them felt inclined to move, nor did they feel inclined to discuss the wisdom—or foolishness—of what they'd just done. If Kate had been privy to his thoughts, she imagined he was, right now, deciding that lust and logic made poor bedfellows and that he should have thought things through with his head rather than with those parts of him that had less control.

Her thinking moved along much the same line, though, from somewhere, deep inside her, came the rogue thought, "*I might still love him.*"

Startled, she sat up in the dark beside him and turned her back on him, clutching her bare knees in the dark. *No. No. No, you don't. You lust after him. Those two things are not the same.*

But what if she was falling in love with him again? What if she'd never really stopped? What if she let him break her heart all over again? Could she even survive that?

On the other hand, what if he didn't break her heart? What if 'they' were...possible?

But he'd said nothing about love. Nothing, ever, about wishing their marriage was anything but a fake. He'd gone along completely with the deception without stipulation. Because he needed her. But love her? No. He'd said nothing about love. They were two lonely people, who needed, *wanted* sex. Nothing wrong with that, except that sex was never just sex with Finn. Intimacy with him was always more complicated than that, all tied up with...*feelings*.

Sometimes...*often*, over the years, she would remember that day he'd walked away from her. The tender words he used, the devastation she'd felt, like a scratched CD stuck on repeat. She'd hear those words every day when she was doing something completely routine, like drying her hair or washing dishes. "*I wish to God things could be different,*" he'd said. "*I'm so sorry, Kate. But I have no choice here.*" But he'd had a choice and he made it. And she couldn't make him shut up now. And she couldn't make herself stop remembering. Maybe he'd been able to forget, but she hadn't.

Now, he touched her back with the warm palm of his hand, sliding it down to her hip where he caressed the cooling curve of her body. "Hey," he said softly. "You cold?"

She shook her head. But she was, suddenly. Cold as hell.

"Wanna go in? We could share my bed. At least until morning before the kids get up."

Again, she shook her head. "That's not a good idea."

He sat up beside her. "Or maybe it is." His voice was low and husky with the promise of more of what they'd just done.

Kate tugged her skirt down and shrugged into her tank after she found the silky thing halfway off the edge of the platform. Finally, she gathered up her underwear and turned to him. "This was fun." She pulled his hand to her mouth and pressed a kiss against his palm. "Really fun. But...don't ask me to share your bed. Okay? I've already broken one rule tonight. A biggie. Don't ask me to break another."

"Kate—" he began with a frown of concern.

"Oh, c'mon, let's not spoil things by getting all serious. And let's not kid ourselves and try to make this mean something that it didn't. We had great sex. We're grownups. We can handle a little indiscretion. Right?"

"Yeah," he said, looking a little wounded. "Right."

"All right then." She kissed him, a quick peck on the mouth, nothing more. "It really was nice, Finn. See you tomorrow?" She sent him her best big-girl smile and climbed down the ladder. It took every ounce of willpower not to stay with him there. Not to wrap herself around him and hold on for dear life. But that wasn't her. Not even close.

In her small, ugly bedroom, she sat alone for a long time on the edge of her bed, staring at the green shag carpeting on the floor, wondering *what was wrong* with her? Clearly, her sisters were right. She *was* messed up and their intervention had been wholly appropriate. She *did* have a problem. Less than a week here and she'd already done what she'd promised herself she wouldn't do. No matter that she'd done the deed with the man who'd once been the love of her life. No matter that he'd made her feel beautiful and wanted tonight.

She'd gone there. Now what? How would they pretend what they'd done hadn't happened? She, for one, couldn't. The worst part was she wanted more. She wanted him in her bed tonight, holding her. The temptation to give in to his request to share his bed had made all her other failures pale in comparison.

What she really needed was a keeper. No, what she really needed was a reality check. Or...a safety hatch.

She picked up her phone and scrolled through her old emails until she found the one she wanted. After staring at the message for a full minute, she typed in a short paragraph, took a deep breath and pushed 'send.'

TWO DAYS LATER, Finn flew to Springfield for his last event until the Copper Mountain Rodeo at the end of the month. He and Kate didn't discuss what had happened between them. In fact, he'd made himself scarce, as he had earlier in the week. Staying away wasn't what he wanted. But he guessed, from the way she avoided his eyes when she talked, that was what she wanted.

He couldn't figure her out. One minute, she was fine and the next, she was pulling away. She was driving him crazy. There was no *changing* the past. Nor would he, if he could. Regrets were a waste of time. Without those broken roads he'd taken in his life, he wouldn't have his children. Or the ranch. Or a second chance with Kate right now. But from the looks of things, he'd done something to blow it with her. The sex had been good. Better than good. No, something else kept her hiding behind those walls of hers. And he was beginning to wonder if he'd ever find a way over them.

He stared out over the indoor arena, jam-packed for the final round of bull-riders that had started less than an hour ago. A dull roar of noise came from the stadium. The pungent odor of animals and the sweaty smell of fear and anticipation permeated the temporary back pens where the riders who'd already completed their rides hung out, watching the competition on closed circuit television. He only knew a handful of them and was fine with that.

He'd scored high in the short go round and for the finals tonight he'd drawn a top rated bull—High Jinx—which, he knew from experience, was both a blessing and a curse. That bad boy had bucked off every rider but one in the last twenty rides and if he kept that up, he'd be well on his way to making the Built Ford Tough Series World Finals in Las Vegas in December as one of the top athlete bulls. Finn just didn't particularly want to help him along. But a good ride on High Jinx meant a high score and that, he needed to win.

"Heard you drew the devil himself," said a voice from behind him.

He turned to find his old friend, Brody Walker, standing beside him. Brody was a two-time world bull riding champion and one of the toughest riders he knew. Already here, he was ahead in points, but not too far to catch. They'd known each other since the two of them were practically kids and enjoyed a healthy sense of competition, but also friendship. He was one of the nicest guys he knew on the circuit, but he never underestimated Brody's potential to steal prize money away from him.

"Yeah," Finn said. "I'll give ol' High Jinx a run for the money, though."

Brody slapped him on the back with a big smile. "I won't say I don't wish I'd drawn him, 'cause I do. I got a bone to pick with High Jinx after the last time I rode him. Threw me at seven point nine-five." He shook his head. "You ever been on his back before?"

"First time."

"Well, you want my advice? Keep in mind, that old joker will move into your hand outta the chute, but then he's just as like to turn back on ya and spin you down the well if you ain't careful."

"Thanks for the tip," he said. "I'll keep that in mind. You on Ghost Dancer?"

"Yeah. Rank bastard. But you might as well go home right now, buddy, since I got this one all sewed up."

Finn laughed. "We'll see about that, pal."

Brody flicked a quick look into the stands and for the first time, Finn wondered if nerves were working on him. "Janie's here with my girls. They're up there in the stands." He gestured proudly up to the section, pointing them out. "Man. I do love that woman. You know what I mean?"

He did.

"You bring your kids?" Brody asked.

He shook his head. "Not this time." Brody had met them twice, but on the street, coincidentally, never at an event.

"Yeah. Makes me a little nervous, too, havin' 'em here. So, what's your excuse? What's got you so distracted anyhow?"

Was he that easy to read? He must be slipping. "Me?"

"Got that *miles away* look in your eye. And that ain't a good thing, my friend."

Miles away with Kate and the twins. This was why he was giving bull riding up. Even Brody could see it. Past times, nothing could have broken his laser-like focus when competing. But his plate was full of pieces teetering on the brink, and he was the only one who could catch them if they fell. "I've got a lot on my mind, I guess," he admitted.

"Get your head in the game, my friend. I intend to win this fair an' square from you."

"Cowboy up," Finn told Brody with a grin.

The other man touched his hat brim with a smile that was always full of mischief. "We'll have a beer when this is done. I wanna hear what's got you so all fired tangled up. But I'm up first. I got my lucky thirteen cents in my pocket. We'll see who comes out on top."

"Only thirteen?" he replied with a grin. "I got at least a quarter."

Brody smiled back. "Luck, man."

"You, too." And he meant it.

"CUTTER, CAYLEE, THIS is Monday," Kate said, introducing Jake and Olivia's sweet dog, who couldn't seem to get close enough to the twins to lick them thoroughly. The kids laughed and hugged Monday around the neck until, panting with dog happiness, the animal surrendered and rolled over onto her back for belly rubs in the grass beside the gazebo at Marietta's Crawford Park.

Monday had the profile of a German shepherd and the buff, grey-point coloring of a Siamese cat. Jake had found her as a puppy in Afghanistan when he was a rescue helicopter pilot, and brought her back from there after recovering from the wounds he'd received there. She was nothing short of a love-bug now and clearly deprived in the miniature person category.

"I think you'd better get her some of those," Kate advised, gesturing at the children. "Chop, Chop. You two are not getting any younger."

Olivia cast an assessing look at Jake. "I know. I plucked a grey hair out of his head today. Just the opening salvo of a landslide of decrepitude closing in."

"Hey—!" Jake complained, curling an impressive bicep for their mutual benefit.

"*Oh.*" Olivia patted his arm. "Well, in that case, maybe there's still a little time. That is, after we get that pesky wedding behind us."

They'd been engaged for four months, but that wasn't enough time to plan a summer wedding, which Olivia wanted. So they'd put the event off until the next summer. But she'd moved in with him in the meantime and that seemed to make life doable for them both.

Jake leaned in to Kate. "That's the first and last time you'll hear her say the words 'wedding' and 'pesky' in the same sentence."

Olivia tsked. "He loves the whole wedding planning thing. Oh, yeah. Napkin choices? We just can't stop going back and forth." To which Jake shook his head behind her, making both Olivia and Kate laugh.

With a kiss on Jake's cheek, Olivia turned to her sister. "Speaking of time passing—"

"Were we?" Kate asked, innocently.

"—Jaycee is already suspicious of what's going on with you and I'm not sure how much longer I can hold her off.

She actually asked me about you the other day after stopping by your empty apartment one evening and I had to…hedge. Of course, they're going to the Copper Mountain Rodeo barbeque dinner and dance in town next weekend and expect that you'll be sitting with the rest of the family."

"A barbeque!" Cutter crowed, apparently listening to every word. "I *love* barbeque!"

"I *hate* barbeque," Caylee said, sinking into an unreasonable pout. Her brother rolled his eyes.

"*What?*" Olivia gasped. "That's practically impossible."

"Caylee prefers vegetables to meat," Kate informed her.

"Ohhh. Well, guess what? They have vegetables there, too. Lots and lots. And dancing. And pretty things to wear."

Caylee brightened. "Can I wear a twirly dress?"

"Ugh," groaned Cutter and his sister sent Kate a secret grin over Cutter's annoyance.

"Only if you promise your dad a dance after dinner," Kate said. Caylee, for one, looked ridiculously pleased with that idea.

They ran off to throw the ball for Monday. When they were out of earshot, she said to Olivia, "We haven't even discussed attending yet."

"Of course you will. You have to. Finn's riding in the rodeo."

"But Dad and Jaycee don't know anything about us yet."

"My point."

"Don't you think it's better if we just keep everyone on

the dark about this whole thing? I mean…there's no need to upset everyone for nothing."

"*Is* what's between you two nothing?"

Kate's gaze fell on the twins, who were tugging the ball from Monday's mouth and whose giggles and smiles had already slipped inside her heart to a place she kept private, a place that squeezed hard at the thought of leaving them. She squinted off at the courthouse—away from Olivia's and Jake's searching looks.

Dark clouds had suddenly begun to gather in the distance over Copper Mountain and she thought of Finn driving home from the airport in bad weather. She'd texted him last night after the event and hadn't heard back, which she assumed meant bad news. She was already worried about him. But she couldn't have it both ways. She couldn't want him to share his life with her if she wasn't willing to do the same in return.

So *was* their fake marriage nothing? Her throat clogged unexpectedly. Yes. Nothing permanent, anyway. And while their made-up relationship lasted, she was…she was—what? Not going to let it change her?

It already has, a small voice informed her. *Too late.* Because she'd had a taste of something sweet and whether she deserved sweet or not, whether she was the type of girl who could stick around for that kind of solidness, the possibility of such a thing had crept in and settled around the place that still protected a seed of hope for such a thing.

"Kate?"

She turned back to Olivia, who was watching a woman who'd been walking across the park, stop and talk to the twins.

Kate knew instantly who she was.

"Oh, hell, no. Excuse me," she said and ran toward the twins and the woman who'd walked out on them four years ago.

Chapter Eight

"CUTTER! CAYLEE!" KATE refrained from screaming, but the words came out as imperatives.

She reached them just as Monday had placed herself protectively between the kids and their long-lost mother. They jerked a look at her in alarm and when she reached them, she grabbed them both by the shoulders and turned them toward Olivia and Jake. Melissa, who'd been crouched beside them, stood then and glared at Kate.

"Jake is missing Monday and he wants to show you a trick. You two go on over now."

"But," Cutter said, "we were just talking to—"

"I know. It's all right. You go on over there now. Both of you."

Melissa shoved her hands in her pockets as they hurried toward Jake with the dog, then turned her scowl on Kate.

Up close, she was still—perish the thought—pretty, but with an edge like a knife blade. She didn't do much smiling, or if she did, it was the kind that was muted by Botox.

"What the hell do you think you're doing?" Kate demanded.

She had the nerve to look affronted. "Talking to my children."

This was bad. This was very bad. "What did you say to them? Are you stalking us?"

"Kate, isn't it? The '*nanny*'? I suppose they don't know who you really are, either."

Cold fingered down her spine. "What's that supposed to mean?"

Melissa shrugged. "C'mon, Kate. We both know you're no nanny. So why the subterfuge with the kids?"

A thousand retorts flitted through Kate's mind, but she weeded all of them out as potentially disastrous. So she said, "I don't owe you any explanations, Melissa. Stay away from the kids." She turned to walk away, but Melissa spoke again.

"Does he know you took that teaching job in Missoula?"

Kate turned and blinked in shock. No one knew. Not a single person except for the principal of that school, whom she'd sworn to secrecy.

"How's that gonna work with your 'marriage'? Not to mention raising the kids together, which apparently was the whole point. Wasn't it?" Melissa was smiling now, the same way she had on the street that day when Kate had run blindly into them. Like she'd won.

"Did you hack me? *Did* you?"

A thin smile curved her mouth. "I have resources, Kate. And not just money. My new husband—"

"—must not give a damn that the woman he married was the kind who would ditch her own children for a party life."

Melissa's expression flattened. "And you're so perfect. That must be why Finn chose me over you."

Instead of backing away, Kate stalked toward the woman, who glanced around her before she began to back up herself. "You don't know who you're messing with here, Melissa. If you think you can go around snooping into our lives, you're dead wrong. My father is a very, very good attorney. Or did your little snitch miss that? He will pin your ass to the wall if he finds you've illegally invaded my privacy or—"

"Is any of what I just said untrue? No?" She laughed. "Good luck suing me for speaking the truth. And do you think the judge will really care once he finds out you both lied to him?"

Kate managed not to slap that silly, condescending grin off her face, but just barely. "That's what all this about, isn't it? Winning? You can't bear that Finn is a wonderful father and you're a pathetic excuse for a mother. Did you ever once call them on their birthdays? Send them a present at Christmastime or even a card? Ever even *try* to visit them before deciding to yank them away from everything they know and love? You never even asked him if you could visit them. He wouldn't have denied you. You know that, right? He would have let you see them any time you wanted. Because that's who he is."

Melissa cocked her jaw stubbornly at her. "You don't know anything about me. Or what I've been through."

"What *you've* been through? Oh, poor you! What about what your children have been through without their mother? Or Finn, raising them single-handedly? That man is a *rock* for those kids. He's loves them more than anything in this world. He's the *only* thing standing between them and that crack in the world that you left behind for them."

Melissa turned and started to walk away, but Kate grabbed her arm, not finished yet.

"Do you get that?" she asked. "They're not pawns in your little game of '*I win*'. They're *children*. They have feelings and little hearts and they need him every day. *Every* day. I don't care if you *are* sober—so you say. I don't care if you have all the money in the world. You can never give them what he can. If you care, even a little bit for those children, you'll let this thing go," she told her, her voice rising. "You'll talk to him like a reasonable *human being*. You'll do what's right for someone else, instead of for you"

Melissa's blue eyes flashed with cold anger. "That's quite a speech, coming from the woman who's about to ditch those same children and her new husband herself. You always did think you were better than me, but you know? We're kind of cut from the same cloth. Aren't we?"

Kate inhaled sharply, the blow of her words hitting her squarely in the lungs.

Her sister appeared at her side, taking her arm before she could do something she regretted. "Okay," Olivia said softly. "Okay. Let's get out of here, Kate."

Melissa, having no more skin-flaying blades left to fling, turned on her heel and walked away. Rain began to fall in big, fat droplets, splatting on Kate's arms and face.

Kate opened her mouth to shout after Melissa, but no words came out. Instead, a dark panic swamped her, stealing her breath and making her heart race. She clapped a hand over her mouth and her eyes brimmed. If what Melissa had said hadn't cut so close to the bone, she would only be angry right now. But the woman's words had found Kate's soft underbelly, the place she protected and tried to keep to herself. Worse, she was absolutely right.

The rain began to fall in earnest then, but Olivia stayed right beside her. "Hey. Deep breaths. Are you okay?" she asked, taking Kate by the shoulders.

She shook her head, ignoring the rain, unable to take in oxygen. "No. No. No. I've ruined everything, Liv. But—*oh, God*—I didn't mean to." Tears tumbled down her cheeks. Tears she could not control. Sobs erupted from someplace inside her she'd forgotten was even there.

Across the way, she could see Finn's children watching her with concern from the shelter of the gazebo. Jake was doing his best to distract them with the dog.

"Oh, Kate. Of course, you didn't. I...I mean, don't be silly." Olivia put an arm around her shoulder, then pulled her into a hug. Both of them were soaking wet in a matter of moments. "You haven't ruined anything."

But she had no idea. No idea at all that Kate had single-handedly sunk Finn's chances to keep his children.

WHEN SHE'D ONLY wanted to run back to Finn's house to hide, Olivia and Jake insisted on dragging her and the children out to lunch at the Main Street Diner. She supposed Olivia was afraid to leave her alone, soggy wreck that she was. She couldn't admit or even try to explain what she'd done. What would be the point? So they could agree with Melissa about how selfish she had been? How she'd simply given in to her impulsive nature without thinking of the potential consequences?

But how could she have imagined the lengths to which Melissa would go?

To make matters worse, Olivia was…*Olivia*, who didn't pry. She simply made her support clear, careful to say nothing in front of the kids. Kate didn't deserve a sister, much less a friend, like her. Deserving a man like Finn was another matter altogether.

She tried to remind herself why she was in this mess in the first place. Because of him. Because of a mistake he'd made years ago. But hating him in the abstract, from far, far away was much easier than hating the flesh and blood man who held her at night and told her he wanted her to stay.

When they'd finished eating—food Kate couldn't even look at, much less touch—and the rain had stopped, Olivia had hugged Kate at her car.

"I don't know exactly what happened out there, but listen to me. Don't you forget," she'd whispered in her ear. "You are in charge of your life, Kate. Not Melissa, not even Finn. When you live in '*what could happen*,' you miss out on all the good stuff that is right in front of you. Listen to your heart, not fear. In my experience, your heart will never steer you wrong."

Easy for you to say. Her heart seemed to do nothing *but* steer her wrong.

Now, she sat at home—Finn's home—trying to drown out that fearsome little voice that always grew louder and bolder than the one that preached bravery. She had to tell him. There really was no choice. But she dreaded his reaction. Once this deception came out to that Missoula judge—and it would—he would look like a liar to the court, despite the fact that the *only* reason he'd married her was for the sake of his children, which *was* the whole point. But the job she'd kept from him was somehow, even worse. A much more personal lie that would drive the final nail in the coffin.

We're kind of cut from the same cloth. Aren't we? Melissa had accused. Was she right? Was she simply in denial that her habit of running from men was any different from what Melissa had done? Were the lies and half-truths she told not self-preservation, but simply a sign of a much darker issue?

Oh, what a tangled web we weave...

Finn's truck pulled into the driveway a little after three p.m. and she jumped up at the sight of him. Relief that he was back after a long radio silence momentarily superseded her worry about herself and the mess she'd created, and she called to the children.

They were at his truck door before he got it open. Through the driver's side window, Kate could see the weary look on his face. The tough weekend and a long flight home showed on his face. But his eyes met hers with something even heavier than weariness. Something had happened. A chill ran through her.

Not until he stepped out of the truck did she see the neon-green cast on his left arm. *Oh, no.* His movements were stiff as he reached for the children to pull them into a hug.

"Daddy!" Cutter exclaimed. "We're twins now! Did you break your arm, too? What happened?"

"Just a fracture, like yours, Snip. No big deal. You like the color?"

Cutter and Caylee were all over him, then, dragging his suitcase between them and herding him into the house. When he reached Kate, who was staring at him in dismay, he reached out and put his good arm around her shoulder, dragging her along with the pack—a gesture the children didn't miss, or seem to mind.

"I'm okay," he murmured. "It's nothin'."

"Oh, Finn. It's not nothing." Kate leaned her head

against his chest and threw her arm around his waist. "I'm sorry. Why didn't you call me?"

"I didn't see the point in worrying you."

She sent him a '*really?*' look. "The point is, you should know better than that. I was worried when I didn't hear from you last night."

"It was complicated. I'll tell you what happened later." He pulled souvenirs from his bag for the twins, a toy bull for Cutter and a rodeo princess pink t-shirt for Caylee. After a few minutes of the two peppering him with questions—which he seemed to answer with extra care—they disappeared with their treasures into the backyard to entertain themselves on the wooden swing he had hung from the tree for them.

"What happened?" she asked when the kids were out of earshot.

He braced his elbows on the sink, looking out the window at the twins. "This," he began, shrugging at his arm, "is nothing. A little inconvenience."

Bracing herself, she waited for more.

"Right before my ride, a friend of mine, Brody Walker, had a bad wreck with the bull he was riding and got hurt pretty bad. He got whipped down onto the bull's horns, knocking him out, then got hung up, pulled into the well and nearly killed. The bullfighters couldn't get him loose. It was bad. He was in surgery most of last night and I was at the hospital with his wife and daughters after they patched me up."

"Oh, no…" She couldn't help but picture that happening to Finn and she tried to keep her gaze from falling to his casted arm.

"I almost didn't ride. Probably should have withdrawn and gone to the hospital with him right then and there. But that would have been bad form. My mind wasn't in the game and this is the result," he said, indicating his broken arm. "I made nearly eight seconds, before High Jinx took a bad spin on me and I lost my balance. He stomped on my arm for good measure and the rest of me feels like I went through the blender. But that's nothing compared to Brody. They airlifted him to Boise this morning. He'll likely never ride again. They're frankly hoping he'll walk."

She exhaled an in-held breath and thanked God that he wasn't the one nearly killed. Did that make her a bad person? "He must be a good friend. That's awful. I'm…I'm so sorry, Finn."

He turned his back to the counter and leaned a hip there tiredly. "Losing the money feels kind of inconsequential right now. But as far as this place goes, it's not. That means I still have to do Copper Mountain Rodeo."

"But your arm—!"

Weary, he shook his head. "That's my free hand. As long as I can manipulate the rope to release my other hand if I need to at the end of the ride, I'm good to go. I just need to…clear my head. Get my focus straight. I let myself get distracted in Springfield. That won't happen again."

She didn't want to think about him on a bull right now. Frankly, the whole thing made her feel a little nauseous, with him landing inches away from something much, much worse. But she felt suddenly clear about one thing: distracting him now about what had happened with Melissa might just be a fatal mistake.

"Let's not talk about that now. C'mon." She extended her hand to him. His warm fingers closed around hers as he moved away from the counter, real slowly, beside her. She studied his movements. "See that? You're in no shape to be thinking about riding again right now. You need to go lie down and get some rest. Even though you're too stubborn to admit it, I know you're in pain right now."

"Nah, I'm all right," he said, but she could tell he didn't mean it. He wasn't all right. Not even close. His friend's wreck and his own brush with disaster had etched a haunted look in his eyes. She'd never known him to lose confidence in the arena before, but seeing your friend nearly killed was more than enough to mess with the head-game required to climb on the back of a two-thousand-pound bull.

Now was not the time to tell him about her disastrous encounter in Crawford Park. She would have to wait until he'd had a chance to get his feet under him again before pulling the rug out from under him the rest of the way.

Then he did something that caught her off guard. He pulled her up against him and hugged her, tucking her head beneath his chin and sliding the fingers of his good hand into her hair. Kate closed her eyes, and tightened her arms around him, inhaling the manly scent of him, wishing things could be different.

"I know things haven't been…easy between us," he murmured against her hair, "or uncomplicated, but this weekend reminded me that I can't take anything for granted. Like time. Or you. I don't want to fight with you, Kate. I don't want us to take to our separate corners and pretend there's not something else going on here."

There were a hundred things going on here, she thought, none of which she could even mention. She pressed her forehead against the strong plane of his chest.

"Whatever is standing between us," he went on, "I want us to put that behind us. I know you didn't sign up for a real marriage, but I want a chance at that. No, don't pull away. Just listen for a second."

She settled against him as tears threatened and guilt clogged her throat.

"I know you care about the kids. They're crazy about you. Maybe you could even come to love them."

"Finn—"

"Maybe you could even forgive me. But if we keep backing away from each other this way, nothing will change."

"What are you saying?"

"I'm saying that I want to give you and me a chance."

At his words, her heart leapt and raced ahead, only to

sink again at the thought of what he'd say when she told him what she'd done.

Timing. Timing was everything.

"I know I'm not wrong in thinking you still feel something for me, Kate. What happened the other night, outside, you can't deny that." His thumbs brushed against her back in a slow circle.

Heat stirred inside her like an eddy at his touch. Oh, yes. She felt. She wanted. She wished for more than he even imagined. But none of those meant anything now. They were all based on lies. Lies and secrets she couldn't seem to help keeping. "It's…it's so much more complicated than what happened out there."

His sweet breath fanned her face, warm and steadying. And he pressed his lips against the crown of her head in a long, lingering kiss—the kind husbands must give their wives. The kind of kiss that meant "I've got you. I'll protect you." The sort of kiss she didn't deserve.

"It doesn't have to be complicated," he murmured. "Only if we make things that way. Putting our past aside can be as simple as taking things one day at a time. As simple as saying *yes.*"

If only the answer was that easy.

Her impulse was to run. Exit stage right before the wheels fell off the cart. But saying 'yes' to Finn was something she'd already done—albeit on a temporary basis. And only now, when she'd already done that kneejerk, irrevocable thing, did he ask her for more.

The irony didn't escape her. But to admit what she'd done to him now, when he was already down and needed all his confidence for the Copper Mountain Rodeo, would be unforgiveable. She couldn't be responsible for him losing that, too. Or, ultimately, everything he'd hoped for on this ranch.

No, she would have to find a way to repair the damage she'd done on her own and try to fix things. Somehow.

With his arms still around her, she spread her fingers against the corded muscles of his back, wishing she could be that girl he used to know, but knowing that was impossible. "All right. Let's call a truce, then," she said softly. "Let's just pretend we both believe in a happily ever after—" *whatever that means*—"and just enjoy the time we have."

If that was her last gift to him, she decided, so be it. Even if she withdrew her name from the job in Missoula—which she would do on Monday morning—it was already too late. The damage was done. The court could only see their 'marriage' as an attempt at deception—which was certainly true—and rule accordingly. Once Finn learned what she'd done, and he'd lost everything he held dear, he rightly would blame her. There would be no reconciliation between them. No pretending there could be a happy ending. But she'd known that all along, hadn't she?

THAT NIGHT, AFTER the children were fed and long asleep and she and Finn had said good-night, Kate lay in her bed alone, tossing and turning, unable to sleep. Every sound in the quiet house was amplified and after they'd both been in bed for an hour, she heard his shower go on.

She sat up with a frustrated sigh. Longing, deep and impossible, rippled through her as she imagined him, wet and naked. There really was no point in doing what she was thinking of doing, except to make things harder. On the other hand, how could things be harder than they already were? But he was right about one thing: taking to their separate corners was getting them nowhere.

Quietly, she left her room and made her way to his. She heard the sound of his shower and as she made her way closer, and through the bathroom doorway, she could see his casted arm, wrapped in plastic, braced against the wall of his shower. His head was down and the water sluicing over his strong, beautiful body was not steamy, but cool, leaving his skin chilled with goose-flesh.

She inhaled sharply at the sight, feeling like a peeping Tom, but unable to tear her eyes away. Everything about him was beautiful, from the curve of muscle in his bicep to the strong lip of his lats, carving a line down the cage of his ribs. He stood with one knee bent, braced against the wall, and her eyes fell to the many scars his encounters with bulls had left on him. There, on his shoulder and another in the small of his back near his hip where bruises from this latest ride also marked him in purple and blue.

And then, he lifted his head and saw her.

Surprise warred with heat in his golden eyes and his pupils grew dark as she moved toward him. The nightgown she wore slipped off and puddled on the floor.

His lips parted, watching her walk toward him. With a flick of his wrist, he changed the temperature of the water as she opened the glass door of the shower and stepped inside. Swallowing thickly, he took in the sight of her nakedness with a longing that stirred him down below with a quick flicker of movement before he pulled her up against him to drop his mouth on hers.

Hungrily and with abandon, she kissed him back, wanting him to understand everything she meant by that kiss and all the things she could never say. The kiss was an apology and a wish at once and she melted into the delicious press of his mouth on hers. His tongue breached the seam of her lips on her invitation and danced with hers.

With his one good arm, he tugged her up hard against him, his fingers spreading across her skin like fire. Steam rose from the hot water pouring down on them, but that couldn't begin to compete with the heat that stirred between them.

His touch made her ache. Every female part of her begged for his attention. And almost as soon as she had that thought, he did just that, dropping his mouth on her beaded nipple while kneading her other breast with his good hand. And he drew her nipple into his mouth until she felt her knees go weak and he pressed her back against the warm wall of the shower.

"Ah, Kate...I thought for a second I conjured you up," he said, puckering her skin with a trail of kisses, making his way toward her belly.

"I couldn't sleep," she said, threading her fingers into his wet hair. "And I see, neither could you."

"Something chronic since you came back in my life." He ran his hand down the side of her hip and traced the shape of her thigh toward the juncture of her legs. When his fingers found her hot, slickness there, a low animal sound stirred in his throat.

She hissed in a breath and tucked her leg around his hip, giving him access and a way to ease the ache he'd discovered. "I'm sorry," she whispered against his hair, but she meant she was sorry for so much more. "What about your arm?"

"Shhh," he murmured, lifting his head and watching her expression shift into surrender as he touched her there. She tilted her hips against his hand to ease the ache he was stirring. A smile curved his mouth and she closed her fist around his velvety hardness, giving him a sweet taste of his own medicine. She stroked him with a fierce tenderness.

"Ahhh..." he gasped into her ear. "Mercy—" He curved his body around hers like a quarter-moon and she basked in his glow.

"No mercy. That would be too easy," she breathed. "Since rules one, two and three just swirled down the drain."

Against the hot column of her throat, he said, "Technically, the sharing the bed rule still stands since this is a shower. But," he said, sliding another finger inside her, "we can dispense with that forthwith."

She clutched his wrist and held firm. "Ohhh, no. Don't you move."

He chuckled and she felt him sink down, leaving wet trails of kisses down her belly until he reached that spot where his fingers had, a moment ago, teased her. With a last glance upward, he replaced his hand with his mouth.

Her head fell back. *Holy rule breaker!*

She flung her arms backward to support herself, praying she wouldn't slip and fall because the strength in her legs was deserting her. Feeling herself slowly disappear, aware only of that small spot of torture and the flick of his tongue, she wondered why she'd thought this was a bad idea. She couldn't seem to recall any valid reason, whatsoever.

Oh, yes. There was that one, but she wouldn't think of that now, because he was pushing her onto some razor's edge of need, tugging her like a ribbon through the eye of a needle and on the other side…on the other side was—

Suddenly, he was standing, filling her completely—the missing piece of her puzzle. She gasped and nearly came at the exquisite pleasure. An answering shudder tore through him and he stilled inside her, dropping his mouth on hers to kiss away any reservations she might have. But she had no coherent one. Only welcome.

They moved together with the steamy water pouring down on them, slowly at first, then letting the ancient rhythm choose them until the friction ignited between them. Locked together with his good arm supporting her, she came with a fury and cried out into the curve of his shoulder. And he followed her right after, holding her as if he'd never let her go.

There they stood for a long time after, holding one another until the water cooled and their breathing calmed. And then he carried her to his bed, breaking the third rule once and for all.

Chapter Nine

THEY FELL INTO a pattern, over the next week, of hard work during the day and long nights spent together in his bed. Finn found her gone before the sun rose and the children were never the wiser.

When the kids were in school, Kate volunteered to become his left hand in the field. Since fixing the leaky barn roof with his left arm out of commission was out of the question—and even with two good hands, such work might be too dangerous for him to tackle on his own—he turned his attention to the other projects that needed doing before he could bring the stock here. With a rented posthole digger, they managed to build a new bull pen beside the barn for the bull he hoped to purchase with the winnings at Copper Mountain Rodeo.

Together, they cleaned out the hayloft and readied the pens with new watering and feeding troughs. She never complained. Not once.

Nor did the kids want for attention. Somehow, she managed to keep the balance with the kids and the extra work.

And day by day, they seemed to fall in love with her even more. He'd never seen them so happy or content. While they weren't prone to meltdowns, even the few that happened, Kate managed to diffuse with offers to bake cupcakes together or to just sit together on the floor building a Lego spaceship or by reading a book to them. Or, even more likely, with a simple hug.

The tough-chick persona faded away around his children and the girl he used to know returned.

Sometimes, he'd watch her over the heads of his children and wonder how he'd been fool enough to ever let her go? Even if he'd had to share custody of the children with Melissa, being with Kate, letting her mother his children was what should have been from the start. He had made the choice to marry Melissa, thinking he was doing the right thing, not only for her, but for their children. Yet, watching Kate love these babies—who weren't even hers—as if they were her own, only confirmed what he already knew: he'd had another option years ago. He'd chosen the wrong one. A mistake he still wasn't sure he could ever put right.

Though she allowed him to make love to her at night, Kate's reticence to truly let him in, to allow her heart to open to him—those things were his fault. He'd deeply wounded her, broken her heart, even though she'd never admit that to him, even now. He began to recognize the barricades for what they were—protection. Even now, when she'd laugh at something he said or suddenly found that she was enjoying herself, she would change the subject or make excuses to disappear or he'd watch something bittersweet wash over her.

To add to the mystery, Caylee had whispered to him one night, as he'd tucked her into bed, that Kate had cried at the park when he'd been gone. Caylee was worried about her, too. It felt wrong to ask Kate, since she'd offered nothing about the tears herself, but he suspected the meltdown had something to do with him and the situation in which they found themselves now. He wasn't sure what was happening, but he wanted to get to the bottom of what was going on with her.

On the Friday before the Copper Mountain Rodeo, they'd driven into town early to get a few supplies before picking up the kids from school and were surprised to see that Main Street had been transformed into a sparkly showplace in preparation for the dinner and dance that would take place the next night. Banners flew from every light post and flyers graced every storefront window announcing the dinner and dance that would be a fundraiser for the future Children's Pediatric Wing of the Marietta Hospital—a cause he was more than willing to support after what had happened to Cutter. After some discussion earlier in the week, he had talked Kate into being his date.

He'd left her shopping with Olivia while he went to see Ben Tyler, ostensibly to check on how his arm was healing. But he had an ulterior motive.

After Ben quit laughing over Finn's lime-green cast that

matched his son's, and taking a new x-ray to check on the healing, he asked why he'd really come to see him. Because clearly Finn had something else on his mind.

"I want you to give me access to my hand, Doc," he told Ben. "I'm riding in the rodeo this weekend and I might need the use of it. It'll only be for those two nights."

"You're kidding me, right?" Ben said.

"Nope." He drew a finger around the edge of his wrist. "Just cut off the cast around my hand so I can grip the rope if I need to when I'm dismounting the bull. Otherwise, I could get hung up there. This thing—" he said, indicating the cast wrapping around his thumb—"won't work."

"Just...cut off the cast." Ben shook his head. "Do I need to remind you that you have a fracture? That part of the cast gives the bone in your arm stability."

"Okay, then. I'll Ace bandage the thing."

"Not the same."

"I know. But it's only for the weekend. If you won't do it, I guess I can find a hack saw somewhere."

At that, Ben scowled. "You know, I'm not so much worried about the hand as I am about the rest of you coming off that bull. But no. I'll do it. It'll be against doctor's advice. And I won't guarantee you'll have the strength you need in that hand to pull that rope at any rate. That will put a lot of undue pressure on that fracture."

"Oh, I'll pull it. Better than getting hung up and dragged all over kingdom come. Right? Besides, I've got no choice. I have to ride. And I have to win."

"I'm a doctor," Ben said, pulling the electric saw from a nearby drawer. "Of all the reasons I've heard for people to try to sabotage their healing, that one just might take the cake. But you win. It's your arm." He kicked up the power on the saw and the thing gave a high-pitch whine. "But don't say I didn't warn you." As he turned Finn's already-battered cast so his hand faced up, he asked, tugging a piece of straw from his wrist. "What the devil have you been doing with this thing? Using it as a hammer?"

Finn grinned, as Ben dug the saw into the plaster. "What? I wasn't supposed to?"

"THAT ONE," OLIVIA told Kate, who was modeling the fourth outfit she'd chosen at the new boutique on Main Street. "Definitely that one."

Glancing in the mirror, Kate eyed the turquoise Vince Camuto v-neck jumpsuit from all angles in the mirror. "I don't know. Too casual?"

"That color is perfect with your red hair. And if I had your legs, I'd wear it."

"Says the girl with equestrian's legs," Kate teased.

She sighed. "It's all in the perspective." A woman exited the second dressing room and eyed Kate's outfit longingly before she moved along. "See?"

Kate glanced at the price tag and her eyes widened. "Oh.

Shoot. I can't afford this."

"Yes, you can. And if you're short, I'll help you. You look amazing in that and Finn will not be able to keep his hands off you."

"That is *not* the point," Kate told her emphatically.

"Isn't it? My bad." A little cat-like grin tipped the corners of her mouth. "The point is, you have nothing fabulous to wear and you need it. Right?"

"I shouldn't even be going."

"*What?* Of course you should!"

With a last glance in the mirror, Kate said, "I feel like a fraud."

"For being in love with him?" Olivia asked.

"That kind of talk doesn't help."

"The truth, you mean?"

"Oh, who cares about the truth when I've already blown the whole thing. As always. That's part of my charm, isn't it, Liv? Leaving a minefield of destruction behind me?"

"That's not true and you know it. You're the best person I know, Kate and I'm not saying that just because I'm your sister. You're the one who came to New York and sat at my bedside until you knew I would be okay after my riding accident. And long afterward. You were the one who never gave up on my chances to ride again, or on the possibility that I could start over and fall in love for real. And look what happened." She shrugged. "So you've broken a few hearts. They were the wrong ones anyway. But, Kate. It's time to stop running and to start fighting for what you deserve. Why don't you just tell him you love him and get it over with? Why not just come clean about everything? Isn't it time?"

"Because, as if what's happened already isn't bad enough, I can't tank his chances for tomorrow with the truth. It'd be cruel to sabotage him that way just to clear my conscience." She stared out the front plate glass window of the store at the decorations going up on Main Street. "Anyway, I've had Dad's *'special research assistant'* looking into things for me."

Olivia looked alarmed. "You don't mean that Trey Reyes?"

"Um...yeah. That's the one."

"Does Dad know?" Olivia's tone implied that hiring a mobster from the New Jersey shore might have been less dangerous.

"No. And don't tell him." Trey Reyes didn't live anywhere near Marietta, Montana. In fact, he was from Los Angeles, but he'd worked for her father for years on cases that required both discretion and an uncanny ability to uncover the truth. Technically, he wasn't a P.I., nor was he a cop, though she suspected he'd been both of those things at one time. His own history, according to rumor, was as shadowy as those people he investigated, but his past was as off limits as he seemed to be. She knew, because she'd tried flirting with him once and gotten absolutely nowhere. Which was, perhaps, why he hadn't made her empty her entire bank account to hire him this time. There might have been a trace of pity involved.

"I'm getting lost in all the secrets I'm keeping for you, Kate," Olivia admonished crossly. "This has got to stop."

"Well, as luck would have it—or not—the hearing is on Wednesday in Missoula."

"Which means you're going to come clean to him as soon as the rodeo's over, right?"

Dread crept over her at the thought. "I think I *will* take this jumpsuit," she said. "Screw the cost." She disappeared back into the dressing room, avoiding Olivia's sanctioning look. Yes, she would tell him on Sunday, but her confession wasn't something she would discuss with anyone but him. At least she owed him that much.

She pulled her phone out and checked her messages. Nothing from Reyes. She sighed. He'd been working for her for almost a week now. Why hadn't he called her? He'd forbidden her to contact him from her cell, for fear that whoever had hacked her had invaded more than just her emails. But pay phones were practically non-existent anymore and the one she'd managed to call him from was in Livingston. No answer.

As the clock ticked down, it was becoming more and more apparent that no one was going to save her from what had to be done. She was going to have to fess up and take what was coming to her.

Slipping out of the jumpsuit, she pulled her jeans and red silk top back on. She would think about all this tomorrow. Or Sunday, after the finals. For now, she still had one twirly pink dress to find for a certain five-year-old girl.

THE SATURDAY OF the Copper Mountain Rodeo dawned on a perfect day. Rain, the afternoon before, had polished the air, leaving nothing but that sweet scent of Montana drifting on the gentle breeze.

Finn had gone back and forth about letting the twins watch him ride. Especially after what had happened the weekend before in Missouri. But since this might be his last ride, ever, he decided to let them come to the event with Kate. He'd drawn a good bull for this afternoon's ride, named Chile Pepper and he'd relaxed a fraction that he hadn't drawn the bull that had nearly killed Brody last weekend, who'd been assigned to some other rider.

Kate held her tongue about Ben Tyler hacking off his cast, knowing Finn was probably right. He needed use of his hand just in case. But that did nothing to boost her confidence about the day. He needed a win, but first he had to pass the short go, or the prelims.

She remembered from years past, that the day of an event usually found him off alone, mentally girding himself for the upcoming challenge. Bull riding was the last event of the day, but he surprised her by suggesting they all go early so the kids could see the calf roping, steer wrestling and—the event that ultimately stole Caylee's imagination—barrel racing.

From the outside, the four of them could have been mistaken for a family. And, in fact, some of his old friends from days past, did just that when they met her—assumed she was his wife. He introduced her simply as Kate—not as his wife or his children's nanny. She did her best to be gracious and pointedly avoided making eye contact with people she knew. But that was nearly impossible, considering she'd spent most of her life here and knew or recognized nearly everyone in town.

During the calf roping, when Finn went for drinks. Caylee climbed onto Kate's lap and leaned her back against her chest. To wrap her arms around the little girl and imagine she belonged to her felt as natural as breathing. Of course, nothing could be further from the truth. But now and then, against her own counsel, she let herself pretend. That was when she glanced up, and found Finn standing at the end of their row with the sun pouring down on him, looking…bemused. His hazel eyes had gone all dark the way they did when he sent her a private look. And she felt a rush of heat tumble through her.

He looked so damned handsome in his plaid shirt and Levis' and that two-day scruff he always let grow on his jaw for good luck that she almost couldn't catch her breath for a moment. And once he put on those leather chaps for his ride, she'd be toast.

But the emotion she saw in his eyes was the very thing

she'd hoped to avoid, and seeing that look now made tears threaten. His look was one all fathers must get when they see their children happy. A snapshot of memory.

That snapshot included her.

In self-defense, she flashed him a quick smile back, then broke the moment by flagging down the nearest shaved ice vendor.

"I just talked to Janie Walker," he told her a few minutes later, when the kids were all settled in consuming liquid sugar. "Brody's wife. She called to wish me luck."

His friend who'd been injured last weekend. She held her breath. "That was nice of her. How's Brody?"

"He's doing better. Looks like with a lot of rehab, he'll walk again, but his riding days are done."

"That's good news, no?" Everyone knew the sport of bull riding had a short window and when that window closed, the athletes who gave that sport up found other careers.

He nodded. "I was thinking, maybe he'd be interested in running the bull breeding business with me. I like him and I could use a partner, someone to share the work and the responsibility—I mean—once he's back on his feet. Who knows? Maybe he'd be interested. What do you think?"

She blinked. "What do *I* think?" *I think we shouldn't be talking about a future where my opinion matters.*

"Yeah," he said. "I want to know."

She filled her mouth with shaved ice. "I—I don't...that would have to be your decision. I—I'm just the nanny, remember?" she said, glancing pointedly down at the little girl slurping a shaved ice in her lap. "But if you want a partner, then someone who's made a name for himself in the business, like you, sounds like a good choice. And asking him…that's very *kind* of you."

"Kind…? No. I'd be lucky if he said yes."

"Then you should ask him."

He watched her for a long moment, as if he were about to say something. Then, he half-smiled and stared down at the tips of his boots. "Yeah. Maybe I will. Listen, I'd better go and get ready." He glanced at his watch. "I'll see you after, okay?" He had the impulse to kiss her, but he stopped himself.

He started to get up, but she caught his hand. "Finn?"

"Yeah?"

"Have a good ride."

He lifted the tips of her fingers to his mouth and kissed them. "I will."

And her heart stutter-stopped.

"WE'RE IN STORE for a real treat today, folks," said the announcer over the loudspeaker as Finn climbed into the chute where his bull was waiting. *"Some of you might remember him from the PBR circuit, but now he's a local boy, who isn't letting a broken arm stop him from keeping his commitment to ride here today. Finn Scott will be on Chile Pepper! Let's have a big Marietta hand for him."*

The crowd erupted into applause and cheering. That kind of thing always surprised him, with so much time intervening since he used to be somebody. He didn't allow himself to enjoy the recognition. Just another distraction. He simply lifted his cowboy hat and tried to focus on the task at hand.

He'd waited through twelve other riders before his turn came up. As he settled himself down onto Chile Pepper's back, the bull stomped his hooves impatiently and tried to bang him into the walls of the chute. He lifted his leg in time to keep his limb from getting crushed against the thick metal bars. His heart raced and slammed against his ribcage. Adrenaline usually took care of his nerves, but Brody's accident last week had shaken him.

Focus.

"You okay, Finn?" asked Gil Bratcher, the gatekeeper, as he helped tighten the bull rope around Chile Pepper's broad belly.

"Just give me a minute," he answered, flexing the fingers of his right gloved hand under the grip of the bull rope as he wound the strap around behind his hand, then tucked the leather against his palm.

He'd made the switch to a Brazilian bull rope a few rodeos ago, and felt safer with it. Hang ups rarely happened using them because of their design. But they'd taken a little getting used to as the grip started slightly off center instead of directly over the bull's spine. He wondered, absently, if

Brody had used a Brazilian last week and if not, if he would have avoided a wreck.

The countdown clock was ticking. Beneath him, the bull quivered, ready to go. The score to beat was 90.2. Ladd Mitchell had ridden the whole eight seconds, but his was still a beatable score.

He deliberately kept his gaze from the arena stands where his family sat, to stay focused on what he was about to do. But just thinking about Kate in the circle of his 'family' sent warmth spreading through him. Predictably, so did panic at the thought of the hearing next week. But he pushed that worry aside.

Not now. Think about the two thousand pounds of muscle under you.

Remember why you're doing this. Get your head in it.

He pounded a fist against the closed fingers of his hold hand.

With a deep breath, he nodded to Gil Bratcher who pulled the gate open.

Chile Pepper exploded from the chute with a quick left turn, then sun-fished to his right. Finn hung on, touching the bull's sides with the dull rowels of his spurs. He felt the pump of his heartbeat match the slam of hooves against the ground.

Three seconds. Four.

More twists and back-jamming jolts. *Stay up*!

Five.

Damn, you're getting too old for this!

The bull ducked its head and kissed the ground, kicking high with its hind legs. He felt himself being thrown forward and shoved his boots toward the neck to keep his balance. *Hell, no!*

Six.

He threw his arm straight up to straighten himself out.

Seven.

Pain jolted through his left arm. *Focus!*

Chile Pepper spun toward the right as the buzzer sounded and he leaned backward, released the rope and threw his left leg over the neck of the bull. He flung himself off, landing in a crouch on all fours. Or, rather, all threes as he tried, unsuccessfully, to protect his left arm from the blow. But pain shot up his arm all the same.

Time blurred the next few seconds as the bullfighters moved in to keep Chile Pepper from trampling him and a heartbeat later, Finn was jumping out of the way and onto a steel railing as the bull snorted past him and back through the gate.

He exhaled a breath and glanced over at the stands where the kids were sitting. Cutter and Caylee were clinging to Kate's side like they'd been stuck there with glue but they were both cheering. Kate was smiling at him and he lifted his chin in acknowledgement of her smile. As he climbed over the fence, he heard the mike sputter.

"A fantastic eight-second ride for our own Finn Scott on Chile Pepper! That bull sure gave him a run for his money. He tried everything to get Scott off his back but that just speaks to

Scott's bull-riding experience that he managed to hang on for the full eight seconds. For those of you who don't know this bull-athlete, Chile Pepper's ranked up there in the top twenty PBR bulls this year and his owner, Lee Greenfield of Greenfield Farms, is hoping to take him to the Las Vegas Finals in December. After that performance, we can see why. Okay now. Let's see the score."

When Kate and the kids reached him, he was grinning from ear to ear.

"Wow!" Kate said, hugging him. "You did great." But in a whisper against his ear, she said, "But that ride scared me to death."

"I wasn't scared," Cutter said bravely, but with his arm locked around his dad's leg like a flag in a windstorm, Finn had to laugh.

"There you go, Snip. I knew you could handle it."

"Me, too," Caylee piped up. "I wasn't scared either. Not even when you fell off."

"I jumped off," he corrected with a grin. "Which is a heck of lot better than *falling* off."

The scoreboard flickered to life and the announcer said, *"Ninety-one point four! Finn Scott takes the lead in this go-round with that sweet ride on Chile Pepper!"*

"Did you win?" Cutter asked. In the background, another rider burst out of the chute and the crowd cheered, making conversation difficult.

"For now. A few more riders to go," he shouted to Caylee, as the next rider got bucked off, almost immediately, landing hard in the dirt. "This was just the first go round. But we'll keep our fingers crossed for tomorrow, okay?"

He glanced at Kate. She looked flushed with excitement and so damned pretty. Not even the anticipation of seeing if his score stood could equal the full body rush of picturing her in his arms again tonight. He felt a like a teenager when he was around her.

Until much later, he'd have to settle for dancing with her this evening, in front of everyone and not giving a damn what anyone thought of it. He wanted to make an honest woman of her. Or let her make an honest man of him. Either way, he was ready to be done with the charade. Tonight might just be the perfect time to put this fake marriage behind them and commit to something real. Especially tonight, with the hearing coming up in a few days.

That flicker of dread entered his mind when he least expected it, but he pushed his fear aside, unwilling to allow the possibility of failure on Wednesday to take hold. He needed Kate to know that his wanting her was not based on her agreement to help him, but because he couldn't imagine his life without her anymore.

"Why don't you guys head home and get ready for the dinner dance? This might go a little long and the dinner starts in less than an hour. I can drive my truck back home and join you at the dinner after I get cleaned up."

"But we should go together," Kate protested. "We'll just wait for you."

"Don't worry. I'll catch up with you there. I need to wait for all the scores to come in. Besides, as we all know, these two need a head start whenever you're trying to get out the door."

"Okay. If you insist. But you'd better not leave me there, all dressed up and no one to dance with."

"Don't worry about that, darlin'. I'll be there. And we will definitely be dancing."

"Me too?" Caylee asked.

"You first, of course!" he said with a smile and a kiss on the crown of her head. "Now go on you three, get, so I can properly obsess about my rankings."

Kate grinned and winked at him in lieu of a kiss on the cheek. "Good luck."

"Thanks. See you later?"

She winked, correctly guessing he meant, later-later. Oh, he'd see her then, too.

AFTER CLEANING THE fragrance of the rodeo grounds from the children with a quick bath and shower for herself, she managed to chase them down long enough to make them look presentable for the dinner dance. Caylee spun around the living room in her twirly dress, a pink confection that made her feel—in her words—princess-y, and Cutter wore his best blue jeans—namely the ones without holes in the knees and a little color left in them—and a plaid shirt that was a version of what his dad had worn today.

As for Kate, she donned the Vince Camuto jumpsuit and heels with trepidation. The outfit felt a little 'big city' for this small town event, but she couldn't back down now. At least she knew Olivia would approve.

They were practically out the door again when her cell rang. The caller ID had a Los Angeles area code.

"This is Kate," she answered, holding her breath.

"It's me."

In only a few phone conversations, she recognized the sexy baritone voice as belonging to Trey Reyes.

"Oh. *Hello.*" She swallowed hard, still uncertain whether whoever had hacked her had access to anything besides her email, so she followed his cryptic lead by not saying his name. "Um…*anything?*"

"Maybe," was his succinct reply.

She inhaled sharply. A spark of hope was better than none. "What does *that* mean?"

"It means…so far, nothing usable. But I'm following up on a lead which may go nowhere. Don't get your hopes up."

"Can't we go?" Cutter complained from the door. "We're gonna miss the barbeque!"

"This will just take a second, Cutter. You two wait over there." Turning her attention back to the phone, she said, "When will you know?"

"As soon as I know," he replied, "you'll know."

"Okay. Thanks."

He clicked off without saying good-bye. She took a deep breath. What could he have found? She prayed he'd uncover something, *anything* they could use that would help Finn keep the kids. She hadn't wanted to get his hopes up, so she hadn't told him about Trey yet. Maybe he needed some hopeful news. Or maybe that would just make the lie all the worse when Trey's lead turned out to be nothing. She knew better than to hope that Melissa's past, alone, would be enough to keep the custody agreement intact. The court wanted mothers involved in their children's lives. Kate had nothing against that, in principle, but in her humble—if inconsequential—opinion, if Melissa deserved anything after abandoning her children for the last four years, she should have visitation, not partial custody. But if the judge in Missoula was pro-mothers, the key to their winning would have to be something else.

One thing she knew. If there was any dirt to be turned up on Melissa—and how could there not be?—Trey Reyes would find it.

Chapter Ten

MARIETTA'S MAIN STREET had been turned into a twinkling fantasy garden with mini-lights strung from lamp post to lamp post and wrapped around the branches of trees that fronted the red-brick, Western-style storefronts. This town, whose charm already drew visitors looking for a taste of the West, had never looked prettier.

The long, gold-sateen-draped tables, already crowded with neighbors and friends, were strewn with mason jars full of summer flowers and candles that illuminated the sparkles tossed along the tablecloths for an extra bit of shine. The mouth-watering scent of barbeque wafted across the street as people piled food on their plates from the buffet set up on one side, where catering pans full of grilled steak, chicken, grilled vegetables, and potatoes sat nestled beside a colorful palette of salads.

Up at the end of Main Street, in the light-strung Crawford Park, there was a band already set up and playing. Lonnie Black was a rising country star who'd gone to Nashville from right here in Marietta. He was a few years younger than Kate, but even back then, she'd heard of him. And he was good. The music wasn't too loud for conversation down this way, but just right for dancing later. She sent up a prayer of thanks that they hadn't chosen Cree Malone to play tonight. God knew, *that* would be uncomfortable.

Wowed by the sight of the twinkling setting, Caylee spun in little circles while attached to Kate's hand, while her brother tugged her toward the delicious aroma coming from the buffet line.

"Kate!" Holding her arms out, Jaycee Canaday pulled her into a hug and directed them to the places she'd saved for them. "Well, it's about time we saw you! We thought maybe you'd dropped off the planet! Where have you been? You look gorgeous, as always. That color is so pretty on you. Here. Olivia told me to save four seats with us, but—" she grinned down at the twins—"she didn't exactly explain why. Now I see." She reached down to greet the twins. "Hello."

"Thanks, Mom. This is Cutter and Caylee Scott. Guys? This is *my* mom."

Cutter stuck his chubby hand out politely. "Nice to meet you."

"Well! It's very nice to meet you, too, Cutter. And Caylee. What a pretty dress you have on."

She nodded shyly. "Kate bought me it."

Jaycee winked at Kate. "She did, did she?"

"I'll explain later. Right now, everyone's starved. Is…um, everyone here?" Kate asked, dreading the bunch of them firing questions at her.

"They're in line at the buffet. Go get some food. I can't wait to see who the fourth chair is for." With a private wink at Kate she sent them on their way.

Note to self: Next time you decide to keep a secret, do so far, far, far from Marietta.

The buffet was crowded and Kate caught a glimpse of the family far up ahead. She spotted Olivia and Jake and her father, filling their plates. Behind them, several barbeques were still cooking up steaks and the fragrant smoke rose in the night air.

And…was that Cody Hoffman standing beside those two children a few people up? That had to be him. A wave of sadness passed through her. She'd known Cody growing up, but he'd left years ago, after high school, to become an architect. Word was that he'd come back to Marietta to his parents' ranch with his young son and daughter after he'd lost his wife. His daughter looked to be only a little older than Caylee. Maybe they could be friends?

Just as she thought to tuck that thought away for later, she caught herself making plans she had no business making. She probably wouldn't be here long enough to introduce Caylee or Cutter to local friends, or help them really settle into this town. Had she already allowed herself to become too invested in them? To imagine herself raising them?

Probably. Somehow she would protect them from it. Somehow she would make things all right for them when she left.

But the thought of leaving at all scraped against her every nerve and tied her stomach into knots. Tomorrow she would have to come clean to Finn and she had to be prepared for his reaction. But she'd think about that tomorrow. Tonight, they would enjoy the night and have fun.

She fixed plates for the children, Caylee's strictly veggies, and she fixed one for herself, though her stomach was knotted and she wasn't sure she could eat.

At the table, everyone was seated, digging into their food, but they all jumped up to hug her as she returned. Olivia and Jake, Eve, her dad, Reed Canaday, and Ken, Lane's End's favorite foreman. She made introductions all around and the kids settled in to eat.

Eve leaned close to Kate's ear. "So, can we assume I've won the bet? Mind you, I'm not as happy about that as I appear. Though I do like the winning part."

"I'm sorry to disappoint, but no, in fact, you've lost piteously. You see, I'm not dating. This is a job. I'm their nanny."

Jaycee eyed her while slicing up Cutter's steak for him. "This wouldn't have anything to do with what we discussed a few weeks back, would it, regarding a particular...someone?"

"Someone, who?" Cutter asked.

Kate felt heat climb to her cheeks. Naturally Jaycee wouldn't miss that connection. But just as she was about to bumble her way into an explanation, she felt a warm hand on her shoulder. That 'particular someone' was standing behind her smiling.

"Sorry I'm late," he said.

Another flash of flustered heat hit her as she jumped up and introduced him. Finn shook hands all around, drawing wide-eyed looks from everyone but Olivia and Jake, who worked hard at feigning innocence. Finn didn't look nervous at all. In fact, he looked downright happy.

"You must be starving. Will you all excuse us for a minute?" she asked and steered him to the buffet. He had a hard time pulling his gaze from her.

"You look…fantastic." A sexy smile pulled at his mouth, and he slid an arm around her to touch the small of her back. "I love what you're wearing."

She felt his touch like a buzz of electricity, a current of lust that had strung itself between them lately whenever they were within arm's length of each other. His compliment pleased her, not only because the only thing he'd seen her in lately had been her dirty designer jeans and sweaty, pulled-back hair, but because he'd actually noticed she'd made an effort.

"Thanks," she said, as her gaze fell to the way his white linen shirt skimmed his muscled chest, and his tight-fitting denims revealed just the tips of his saddle-leather colored cowboy boots. All she could think was, '*Gah!*' because there wasn't a better-looking man in the crowd. But it was the smile full of promises he flashed at her that sped up her heartbeat. "You look great, too."

He gave her a little squeeze against her hip with the palm of his hand. "So, I like your family," he said, as if meeting them wasn't something he should have done years ago.

"We have to sit with them. Sorry. It's going to be...tricky." Did she just imagine he winced a little? "Are you okay? Don't keep me in suspense! What happened?"

"I'm in first place going into the finals," he admitted with a grin.

"Oh, Finn! Of course, you are!" Without thinking, she hugged him, wrapping her arms around his slim waist. He returned the favor, pulling her up against him. After a moment, she stepped awkwardly back, embarrassed, and looked around to see if anyone had noticed.

He gave a knowing smile, but leaned close to her ear. "I want to kiss you right now."

She blinked up at him, feeling a sharp tug of hunger that had nothing to do with the nearby food. "No, you don't."

"Oh, yeah, I do." His fingers secretly fondled the back of her neck, then slid down her back to just a little south of propriety.

She shrugged his touch away with a private smile. A smile that promised more intimate touches later. "The gauntlet of my family might be safer than standing next to you in this crowd."

"Your family looks pretty harmless to me."

"Don't be fooled by all that fuzzy wool. They're waiting to pounce on you like wolves."

"I think I can handle it."

"That's what everyone thinks. But they show no mercy if they sniff potential."

The line crept forward. "Well, in that case," he said, with a grin, "we're definitely in for it."

Once they got back to the table, the family was laughing at something Cutter had said, while the boy blushed, pleased to be the center of attention. Caylee seemed to be watching the big family with quiet awe.

"I hear congratulations are in order, Finn," Jaycee said, warmly. "We hear you won your round today."

"Thanks," he said. "We'll see how the finals shake out tomorrow."

"That was some ride, man," Jake said.

The others jumped in, ooh-ing and ahh-ing about Finn's eight seconds and the other scary bull rides today.

"Give me a helicopter in a dust storm any day over getting on the back of one of those monsters," Jake said, to which everyone laughingly agreed.

"I've never ridden in one," Finn told Jake. "I guess they're a twitch more predictable than a bull."

"Hey, I'll take you up sometime, if you want a ride."

His eyes widened. "Really? Man, I'd love to."

Olivia sent Kate a private smile.

"How long have you been bull riding?" Eve asked, all

wide-eyed innocence. "And how exactly do you know my sister?"

Kate clucked her tongue with a warning. "Eve!"

"What? I'm just asking."

"Been riding since I was nineteen or so," he answered. "Though, I took a break for a few years. But I've known Kate almost that long."

Eve slid a disbelieving look at Kate. "*Reeeal-ly.*"

"So," Jaycee said, "you and Kate have…known each other since…college, hmm?"

"University of Montana. We met there."

Kate found a fascinating piece of chopped broccoli on her plate to study.

"So, Cutter and Caylee tell us you're their *nanny*, Kate," her father said as she played with her food.

Here we go. "That's true," she said. "Did you tell them about the new treehouse, kids? They're helping Finn build one in a big cottonwood tree in the backyard. It's nearly done isn't it, Caylee?"

Caylee nodded enthusiastically while staring shyly at her veggies.

"And the hayloft?" she continued, before anyone could get a word in edgewise. "And the new bull pens?"

"And the sky in our room," Cutter added, matter-of-factly.

All eyes slid from Cutter to Kate.

"She, uh," Finn began, "painted the kids' room with a

sky. With clouds. And stars. And…all that."

"But sometimes," Caylee added, still staring at her plate, "Kate sleeps with Daddy in his room, because her room is not very pretty like ours."

Silence thundered around the table, like the moment before a tornado touches down or a bomb goes off. Kate gaped at Caylee, her fork halted halfway to her mouth. A curse word bubbled up to her lips. She couldn't decide which was worse, that Caylee knew they'd been sleeping together, or that she'd just spilled the beans here to her whole family. Her gaze darted to Finn, who looked every bit as stunned as she felt.

"Mm-hmm," Eve murmured, leaning closer with the sort of shit-eating grin only a younger sister can generate. "Apparently, *I* win."

Reed shoveled in some food and just stared at the two of them.

"More wine anyone?" Jaycee asked brightly.

Kate thrust her now empty glass out. "Yes, please." *Kill me now.*

"There's a not-so-simple explanation for *another time*," Olivia said, flashing a sideways look at the kids, who apparently were taking the whole sleeping-together thing in stride. Kate gulped down some wine.

"Wait," Eve turned a suspicious look on Olivia. "What do you know about this?"

"People!" Kate said, getting impatiently to her feet. "I'm

a grown woman, in case that has escaped your notice and wherever I happen to…lay my head down at night, is not a topic for family conversation. Period. Finn? Would you please ask me to dance?"

He got to his feet, leaving behind half a plate full of un-eaten food and took her by the hand. "Wanna dance?"

She cast one last censuring glance at her family. "I'd love to."

"YOU OKAY?" HE asked, as they reached the dance floor, already crowded with people. Lonnie Black was singing a country love song about a break-up—w*hat else?*—with his Sam Hunt sexy voice. Couples were slow dancing.

All around her. Real couples, dancing. She was the only fraud here.

"I'm fine." After all, what had she expected from her family? *Boundaries?* Oh, she couldn't blame her family. They loved her. All around that table, they were watching her with real hope for her future happiness. How could she not appreciate that? She did. She just didn't want to see the disappointment in their eyes when she failed, yet again.

"Did you know Caylee knew about us sleeping togeth-er?" she asked him.

"No. She must have come into the room in the middle of the night. It's been their little secret, I guess." He took her by the hand and pulled her out onto the dance floor, tugging her up against him.

"Oh, Finn—"

"Stop worrying. They're resilient and they have no idea what us in bed together really means."

Maybe she was as in the dark as they were. The question of what it meant was one she'd been asking herself for a week now. Sleeping with him. Settling into his life like she belonged… Every molecule in her warned her to run. Run right now before things got even more complicated and awful. What was wrong with her that she couldn't just let him hold her without looking for the exits?

Running, a small voice said, was the coward's way out. And where had it gotten her? Nowhere.

So why don't you stay? Fix things and stay.

"What was all that about Eve winning a bet?" he asked, pinpointing the least important *faux pas* moment of the entire familial debacle.

"Nothing. Really. Just a silly…" She shook her head with a smile. "My family… I love them dearly, and they mean well. But they take a little getting used to."

"It's obvious they all love you," he said. "I envy that. That's a gift, you know. Not everyone gets that."

She cut a look up at him. "I know that. I do. I guess I've…just never wanted to disappoint them."

Brushing a piece of hair from her eyes, he said, "Why would you think they couldn't handle a little disappointment now and then? It comes with the territory, doesn't it? Just like celebrating the good stuff."

But, she thought, there was disappointment and then, there was *disappointment.*

With a laugh, he said, "Come here."

God, he smelled delicious. Soap, a touch of something musky and the essential essence that belonged to Finn alone.

He swung her around with the same athletic expertise he used in the arena, guiding her, matching her step for step, their legs winding together like perfect notes in a song. She pressed her cheek against his shoulder in a very un-nanny-like way, really not caring if anyone knew what they were to each other, or what the next few days would bring.

Nearby, she spotted pretty Kendall Dixon dancing with Brent Ashton, who, she'd heard, had just returned from Australia. Were they together? Suddenly, couples seemed to be springing up everywhere in Marietta. She tried hard not to feel jealous that their lives seemed much less complicated than her own. But then, maybe she was wrong about that, too.

The crowd applauded appreciatively when the song ended and Lonnie launched immediately into another, much rowdier cover song called Copperhead Road, that had a line dancing beat that could not be ignored. Kate laughed as he pulled her into the line beside him and off they went.

He'd always been a good dancer, but he'd claimed to be rusty when they'd talked about coming to the dance. There was no rust anywhere in sight as he expertly followed the complicated steps with her.

Slapping her heels down, she kicked her feet out, the feeling cathartic and angry at once, as the tempo of the song picked up. Through the entire dance, he held her hand and hardly took his gaze off her. She smiled back at him, feeling breathless and wanting to act on that look in his eyes, that hot, I-want-you-under-me look.

Olivia and Jake appeared then, with Cutter and Caylee, who were already dancing in their own unique way with some of the other children on the dance floor. Caylee nailed Finn for a slow dance next, and he held her in his arms and spun her around the floor as she smiled up at him.

Kate danced with Cutter as Olivia and Jake took the floor, looking as in love as anyone Kate had ever seen. Could she be happier for her sister? No. But that didn't make the direction her love life was about to take any easier to bear.

"Are you gonna be our mom?" Cutter asked suddenly as they spun across the dance floor.

Kate stopped dead. "Um…*what?*"

"Caylee thinks you are, but…"

"Oh…Cutter, I…I don't…"

Even a five-year-old could hear the impending doom in the tone of his name spoken *that* way. He shrugged and looked away as the song ended and Caylee bounded up to him.

"Let's go get ice cream!" she chirped. Olivia appeared beside her as the two scampered back toward the tables where Jaycee and Reed were.

"I'll keep an eye on them," Olivia told her. "You two just…dance. Or, do whatever…" She winked as Finn joined her with a smile.

She was still shaken by Cutter's question when Finn pulled her off the dance floor.

They were both glowing in the warm evening. Before they could make a clean getaway, he was stopped by at least four people, congratulating him on the ride. He thanked everyone, good-naturedly, but kept hold of her hand and pulled her with him toward the pathway that wound through the park. They laughed together as they wandered onto the grass, where twinkling lights and paper bag luminaries, filled with sand and flickering candles lined the walkway toward the gazebo.

Halfway there, he stopped and kissed her. Not a hard kiss. Or even a lingering one. Just a kiss that stopped her heartbeat for a nanosecond and made her want more. But, instead, he kept walking, pulling her by the hand.

"Where are we going?" she asked.

"I don't know," he said. "I just want you to myself for a minute."

"We should probably keep our eye on the kids."

"Olivia's got them. There's something I want to talk to you about."

Kate stiffened. Had he found out? But, then why had he kissed her? Did he know what the twins had been discussing together? *Heaven help her.*

He stopped under a tree and drew her back with him against the trunk.

"You're scaring me," she told him.

"Listen," he began, "I know things are...complicated for us. Hell, they've always been complicated. But I...these last few weeks with you have been good. I mean, *better* than good."

"Finn, we need to——"

"I know we started this whole thing off on a lie, but this marriage doesn't feel like a lie anymore. It feels like the truth. For the first time in a long time. This feels right. And you know I'm grateful for what you did. But this...you and me...is not about that anymore. Take the hearing out of the equation for a minute and let's just talk about us."

She felt heat climb into her throat. Strangling. A sound came from her somewhere between a groan and a cry for help. *No. No we shouldn't.* A crowd of people sauntered by, laughing.

"We should talk after the rodeo," she said. "You need to keep your focus on the rodeo."

"Just hear me out," he said, ignoring all the warning signs. "I don't know what's in your head. I never know, because you keep everything so close to the vest, Kate. But I want to. And I know what I feel when you're in my arms. When I wake up with you in the morning and see you there. My kids already love you and I think you're starting to love them. But no matter what happens with this hearing—"

She squeezed her eyes shut.

"We'll get through whatever happens if we're together," he continued. "What I'm trying to say is—"

"Kate Canaday? Is that you?"

One of the women in the passing crowd stepped toward her with a big smile. Judy Elsworth, the Marietta Elementary School principal.

Oh. Dear. God.

Kate had an out-of-body experience, as if she were seeing the scene from above as the woman headed toward her with her hand extended.

"Mrs. Elsworth!" she stammered. "Hi." Coherent words eluded her.

"I'm so happy to run into you, here, Kate! I've been wanting to congratulate you on the Missoula job! It's coming up next week, right? You know, the principal there, Nancy Ruland, was a roommate of mine in college and..." *Blah, blah, blah...*

The woman's words buzzed into a blur as Kate imagined the park, curling up and swallowing her. It was Nancy Ruland she'd sworn to secrecy. She hadn't, in her wildest dreams, imagined Judy Elsworth would out her. She felt Finn's disbelieving gaze bore into her, but she couldn't look at him. She just couldn't.

"Oh. I—I'm *sorry*," Mrs. Elsworth said, as if suddenly noticing the crackle of something in the air between her and

Finn. "I didn't mean to—am I interrupting something? Please forgive me. I just wanted to wish you well, dear."

Kate nodded politely. "Thank you. *So* much," she murmured as the woman stole off with her friends, leaving behind a pitted landscape of misunderstanding between her and the only man she'd ever really cared about.

He stared at her, waiting, his posture stiff. "You took a job? In Missoula?"

"I—" she began. "Yes."

"When were you planning on telling me that? Before or after I asked you to marry me for real? Oh, never mind. Apparently, *after*."

Her eyes filled as she studied the twinkling lights strung in the tree. "We *are* married for real."

"No. Married people live together. They don't secretly take jobs two hundred odd miles away."

"I…" She pressed her palms against her eyes. How could she possibly explain herself now? Now that she'd been outted as a liar. She'd planned her speech for tomorrow, after the rodeo, had her thoughts all prepared, but now…too late for self-protection. For speeches that would somehow vindicate her. "I wanted to tell you, but—"

"But *what*, Kate? You never had the chance? You mean all those nights we were sleeping together in my bed, making love together, never once did you have the chance to say, 'Oh, by the way, I'm taking a job in Missoula. None of this means *anything* to me.' Huh? Never once did it occur to you that there were two of us in this relationship?"

"That's not true."

"What's not? The fact that there are two of us, or that it never occurred to you?"

She deserved that, she supposed. "That it...that we...mean nothing to me. That's not true."

Lonnie Black and his band cranked up a honky-tonk country song about girls in cut-offs and long-neck beer. Couples walked by, hand in hand in sharp contrast to the two of them in a stand-off under the canopy of the maple tree.

He stretched his arms out, palms up. "What do you want me to say here, Kate? That I should have known? That this was our agreement? That nothing changed between then and now? Well, it damn well did. For me, anyway. I thought it had for you, too"

"It did. I *know*. My bad. Okay? I took the job weeks ago, because I was scared, all right? I didn't go searching that job out, it fell in my lap. But yes. I grabbed it. I was terrified of what I was starting to feel for you and...and risking my heart again with you when I thought...when I knew there wasn't a chance for us—"

"You *knew*? Weeks ago? So...what? You were playing me? Was this a game to you?"

"No!"

"You didn't even give us a *chance*. And how exactly did you know then that—?"

"It doesn't matter now. Really. Clearly. You have every reason to hate me."

"*Hate* you?" He looked like he was getting ready to explode. "I don't *hate* you, Kate."

"If you don't already, you will. Trust me. Because…it's worse than that."

His scowl deepened. "What the hell does that mean? Worse than what?"

"Worse than me taking the job in Missoula."

He looked almost afraid to ask. "What else?"

"Melissa knows."

His lips parted as understanding dawned. As the reality of what that meant settled over him. "*How?*"

Kate told him about the encounter at the park with his ex-wife and the hacking.

He turned away from her then, bracing one hand on the smooth bark of the tree and leaning over, trying to catch his breath. "If she tells the judge—"

"She said she already has." Kate stared at the ground. "I'm so sorry, Finn."

"*Sorry?* You didn't think I should know this? To prepare for it? To do something about it? These are my *children* we're talking about. *My* children."

And they would never be hers. Her stomach twisted. Should she tell him about Trey Reyes? What good would that do? If Trey found nothing, her hiring him would simply be another secret she kept from Finn. One more stone on her grave. "With everything on your plate, the ranch, the rodeo...I wanted to try to fix what I'd done on my own."

"*Fix* it? You mean now that the judge knows I planned to deceive the court? Oh, scratch that. That would be you. *I* actually wanted to marry you."

Past tense.

"I withdrew my name from the job. Probably too late to matter. But for what it's worth..."

"For what it's worth..." He shook his head. "You know what your problem is, Kate?"

She lifted her eyes to his, only to find exactly what she expected—that same disappointed look her sisters had given her at Grey's Saloon a few weeks back. That look that said, *'we've tried, but we just can't figure out how to help you help yourself.'*

She lifted her chin, her lips pursed to hold back tears. "No. Why don't you tell me, Finn, because apparently, I can't figure my flaws out all on my own." Actually, she couldn't. He was right.

He stepped close to her, keeping his hands at his sides. Not touching her for the first time in weeks when he'd been this close. "You've never believed in us. Or trusted what we had together. Not six years ago, before you left for Italy and not now. But the real problem is you never believed in yourself. If you had, you'd know that this—" he gestured between them—"you and me, what's between us, is rare. And that doesn't come along often. Almost never. But maybe I was just kidding myself, thinking you could actually forgive the past and love me. Maybe I just saw what I wanted to see."

She took a step back. Out of reach. "I never meant to hurt you. I wanted to help you. But I screwed up. I always screw things up. That's what I do." Her eyes brimmed, but she refused to cry. "You asked what that bet was about? My sisters bet that I couldn't go without a date for a month. And you know why? Because I'd been dating too many men, in their humble opinions. I can't have a real relationship. Every one of those men had an expiration date stamped on his head. Because *I can't do relationships*. So the bet was a dare. And I couldn't even manage to see that through. No, I had to marry you. Not technically dating, but hey! Why not go head-on into disaster instead of just dipping my toe in? Drag your beautiful children into the fray. But we both knew there was an expiration date on this 'marriage.' Didn't we? Which is why I'm just a nanny and not a *real* wife."

He just shook his head helplessly at her. "Seriously? You're gonna play that card? That was how *you* wanted it."

She reached for the gold chain around her neck where the diamond rings hung and tugged it over her head. Shoving the rings in his hand, she closed his fingers around them. "Don't worry. I'll be in Missoula on Wednesday, because I promised I would. And I'll lie for you. I'm pretty good at it, don't you think? Maybe I'll even convince him that we're a real couple. I'm sorry, Finn. Really. I'm so, so sorry."

She turned to go and hurried down the path toward the tables where she'd left her family.

"Kate!" he called after her, the gold chain dangling from his fist. "Dammit!"

But she didn't turn around. Instead, she ran.

UNDER THE DARK, star-tossed night outside his back door, Finn took a long pull of whiskey straight from the bottle and paced the backyard. Midnight had come and gone, and she still hadn't come home. She'd disappeared from the dinner/dance in town like a phantom after telling his children the biggest lie of all—that she had to go unexpectedly out of town, but that she'd be back.

His daughter, the wise one, the old soul, may or may not have seen though the transparency of this excuse but, as he'd tucked her into bed, she'd done her best to hide the tremble of her lip at the thought of Kate's absence, even for one night.

"She's not like Izzy," Caylee had told him, "or any of our other babysitters, is she, Daddy?"

"No," he'd said simply. "No, she's not, darlin'."

She comforted him with a reassuring pat of her delicate hand on his. *Wasn't she the one who needed the comforting?* "Don't worry. She won't forget to come back because she promised we'd make brownies for your birthday."

His birthday? Hell. He'd forgotten all about his birthday

on Tuesday, with everything going on. *Happy freaking Birthday to me.*

"Caylee," Cutter had scolded from his bed. "That was gonna be a surprise." He clapped a dramatic hand on his forehead. "She can't keep a secret."

"Hey, I know a bakery in town that makes pretty good brownies," he said. "Anyway, all I really want for my birthday is you two rascals." He tickled Caylee, who dissolved into a fit of giggles as Cutter dived onto her bed to join in the fun. Finn scooped them into his arms and held them tight, his fear a palpable thing that even they didn't miss.

Cutter pretended to be strangling and flung himself dramatically on the bedcovers, but Caylee cuddled with him. "Should we sleep in your room tonight with you, Daddy?"

He actually considered taking them up on their offer for a moment, then laughed. "Then how am I gonna ride in the rodeo tomorrow when you two hog the entire bed and keep me awake all night?"

They giggled again, busted, as that was exactly what they did when they got the chance. Little pinwheels.

"If you get scared by yourself, you can sleep in here with us," Cutter told him.

Something twisted in his chest. God, he loved them more than a man had a right to love. "I'll remember that, son. Thanks."

"I love our room," Caylee said, hugging herself and staring up at the glow-in-the-dark moon and stars and the clouds that Kate had painted for them. "I always want this to be our room."

"It will always be your room," he promised. "No matter what."

Now, alone in the dark, with fireflies winking in the air and stars wheeling overhead, he felt like running, hard and fast, to burn off this feeling of helplessness. Until sweat poured down him and washed away his anger. Instead, he kicked a fist-sized rock in the dark. Pain shot up his foot. With a dark curse, he picked up the rock and heaved it blindly. The thing rang against a metal fence and thunked to the ground.

Damn. How much had he drunk?

And why wasn't there more?

And where the hell was she? Had she fled out of town? Or was she still here? She'd kept her apartment in town. For a quick exit. A painless good-bye. Maybe she'd known all along this was how things would end between them. He thought briefly of calling Izzy to sit and going to find her, but he couldn't bring himself to go chasing after her. He was too mad for that.

Mad was just a word that didn't explicitly cover what he was feeling now. About how she'd kept things from him. About the job she'd taken without telling him. He had a right to be angry, didn't he? After all, she'd made him think...she'd led him to hope...

Fuck.

How could she not have told him? Not trusted him? More importantly, how had he missed all that? Had he not been looking or just not seeing what was right in front of him?

And Melissa, pulling the strings in the background as if they were all some kind of puppets to be messed with. Even her own children.

He supposed none of that mattered now. Kate was, for all intents and purposes, gone, along with his chances of keeping his children. He supposed the blame was more his than hers. The lie that was their marriage had been his doing, after all, and his best laid plans to convert that lie into truth had failed miserably.

The call to his attorney, Mark Erlewine, earlier that night, did not go well either. Though Mark had been working at his end to make sure they didn't lose, he warned that this new revelation could torpedo their arguments and the Missoula judge would not look kindly upon them. Mark told him to brace himself for the possibility that Melissa would win and that he would lose at least partial custody of the twins.

He sat down on the newly repaired porch swing and took a swig from a bottle of Jack Daniel's, swearing he wouldn't go down without a fight. Tomorrow, he'd win his event come hell or high water and on Wednesday, he'd do whatever it took to keep his kids. With, or without Kate.

Chapter Eleven

K ATE HADN'T PLANNED to come to the finals, but she found she couldn't stay away. Wearing a baseball cap and big sunglasses, she stayed away from everyone who knew her and kept to the back of the arena so there'd be no chance the children would see her.

Of course, she saw *them*. They were sitting near the chute with Izzy, watching the events as they had with her, just yesterday. Imagining the sweet cuddle of Caylee against her, she felt a wave of misery wash over her again as Finn got ready to ride.

Coward that she was, she'd hidden herself away at her apartment last night and hadn't called him. She'd told herself she needed some space to think. But her thinking was a circular loop that always ended back at her, holding the blame. If she'd stayed last night, and not run, would things be different? What was he thinking? Had he written her off? Slept like a baby? Already moved on? No, that wasn't right. She knew he hadn't. The look in his eyes last night haunted her. He'd trusted her and she'd…

I don't hate you, Kate.

He'd said that and only belatedly, she'd heard it. In the middle of the night she'd heard his words and wondered how he had managed to say them right then. On the brink of losing it all?

You never believed in us and more importantly, you never believed in yourself.

He was right. She saw that now. She saw now that she'd spent most of her life protecting herself, her family. Choosing fear over risk. Escape over possibility. She'd sabotaged every relationship she'd ever had, including this one. And for what? Who wouldn't fall for a man like Finn? A man who was *all* heart and *no* fear?

Well, at least she could admit that one thing to herself: she loved Finn Scott. She loved his children. Loved who she was when she was with him. He made her better.

She could admit these things now. Now that they were out of her reach. *Perfect, Kate. Your timing sucks.*

These thoughts—the same awful ones that had plagued her all night—still roiled in her mind as she watched the bull give the back of the chute a stomping and Finn, jump off and begin again, holding his left arm, with its decapitated cast, out of the fray.

As the first place finisher in the first go round, he was the last to ride today.

Already some good scores had been posted. She knew nothing about the bull he'd drawn, Zingo, except for the talk she'd heard around her about the animal. Apparently, the bull was ranked high and had a low tolerance for anything on his back. Which, according to Finn, made for a great ride. Or a bad fall.

The loudspeaker whined and the announcer said, "*Let's hear it again for Finn Scott, folks!*"

The crowd cheered and Finn lifted his hat to them, but kept his head down. She'd wanted a good look at his face, but couldn't get one. Had he slept? Did the dark circles under his eyes match hers? She hoped not.

No, actually, she did.

Some small, awful part of her wanted him to look miserable, or even half as ragged as she felt today. A daisy-fresh Finn meant that she'd been right about last night. That they were well and truly finished.

The announcer continued. "*Coming into this round in first place, Scott will need the full eight seconds and some good scores to win. Ladd Mitchell, who came into this round second has a combined score of one-eighty point three this afternoon, and that has him breathing down Finn Scott's neck.*"

She pressed both fists against her mouth to keep her heart from leaping out as she waited for the gate-puller to do his job. *Please let him win. Please let him win. Please let him win.*

The brown and white spotted, long-horned bull exploded from the chute, wrenching Finn in five directions at once. She gasped, but he managed to stay on, pushing his heels down and forward as he'd always told her he must to stay upright.

Two seconds in, she shoved to her feet.

Three, she sat back down.

The bull sun-fished on him, twisting in mid-air. This bull was tougher than Chile Pepper, but Finn looked magnificent on him, matching him stride for stride. *Four.* What he made appear easy was ridiculously hard. His training from years ago did not fail him now.

The buzzer sounded so quickly she thought there must be a mistake, but Finn jumped safely off the bull and dodged the flying hooves on his way to the rail. The spotted bull tore through the reopened gate like a trained dog.

What a sport! Being a spectator alone could shave years off your life.

"Thought I'd find you here. Hiding behind sunglasses."

Her father's voice came from behind her as he stepped over the bleacher seats to sit beside her. *Oh, no.* "Dad."

He folded his six-foot frame beside her. "We were all worried about you last night. You left in such a hurry. We tried to call, but you didn't answer your phone."

That's because I was screening. "I know." She kept her eyes on the arena and Finn, and held her breath for his scores.

"Look," Reed said, folding his patrician hands between his knees. "Your mom told me what you told her about Finn. And Olivia was cagy about what she knew. So all I can go on here is what I saw between you two at dinner. What I saw in his eyes when he looked at you."

What look was that? A man about to step off a blind edge?

"You're a grown woman. Whatever is going on with you and him, that's your business. But we want you to come over for dinner tonight. You're clearly upset over something. We don't like the idea of your being alone."

Silent, her gaze on Finn, she reached for her father's hand and squeezed it.

He took her hand in both of his, surprised. "What is it, Katie?"

She shook her head. "Finn and I...we broke up. No. Scratch that. I broke up with him."

A frown furled his brow. "But you're here, watching him."

"I am." She turned back to look at Finn, watching the scoreboard, which flickered and Finn's numbers came up. Ninety point four!

The announcer shouted, "*That ride puts him over the top. Our winner, Finn Scott, ladies and gentlemen with a ninety point four! What a ride!*"

As the arena broke out into applause and cheering, she exhaled the breath she hardly knew she'd been holding. He'd won. Good, she thought. *Excellent.* At least *that.* She got to her feet, but her legs felt like they were made of silly putty.

Reed stood up beside her, too, and at that moment, she caught Finn staring straight up at her. Indeed, he still hadn't shaved and the dark smudges beneath his eyes might just be worse than hers. Instead of feeling relief, she wanted to cry.

Then, he touched the brim of his hat to her before turning back to the crowd.

She lifted her chin.

Aaaaand...scene.

Tears welled in her eyes. She turned back to her father, the man who'd survived losing the love of his life, only to find another. The man who'd loved his daughters through it all watched the love of *her* life turn away from her. "I did that," she told him as he pulled her into an unsolicited hug. "I don't—" she went on, messing with the lapels of his sports coat, "I'm tired of running. I want to fix this, Dad. I *need* to fight for him. I love him. I love everything about him. He...he makes me a better person. But I messed it all up. I don't know what to do. What should I do?"

Her dad smiled a smile that looked like it was a long time coming. And when he spoke, his voice was thick. "There's my girl. Come to dinner. We'll talk. We'll help you. That's what family is for."

Her breath caught and she nodded, kissing him again. "Okay." And that one, simple word must have weighed a hundred pounds. "I'll come. I'll see you later. I love you, Daddy."

"Love you more."

She smiled. Before her mother had died, she used to say that to them all the time. Then he'd said it until, Kate supposed, they were too old to need such things. She guessed today, she wasn't too old.

With a quick squeeze of her hand, she left him and started down the bleachers toward the exit.

At the bottom of the arena, standing out in this place full of cowboys like a wolf at a picnic, stood the darkly handsome Trey Reyes, waiting for her.

FINN'S BIRTHDAY DAWNED warm and bright on Tuesday, in direct contrast to his declining mood. On the day before the hearing, everything should be washed with grey. But the world just kept on spinning, dressed in bright colors, even when his personal world was falling apart.

He sipped the strong coffee he'd made and sat on the porch swing, formulating his plan for the day. There was a faculty meeting day at school today, so the kids were off and sleeping in. He would leave late today for Missoula to be on time for the hearing tomorrow. But he'd promised the kids brownies in town for his birthday and to finish up the last of the treehouse renovation. And he didn't feel like doing any of it.

Winning yesterday had done little to mollify the darkness that had settled over him. Oh, winning was a hell of a lot better than losing, and he was grateful for the money and what a win could do for this ranch, but the actual victory left him feeling empty.

Was that because Kate wasn't here to celebrate with him? He wanted to argue against that notion. Common sense and what vague bit of self-protection he still clung to warned that he needed to let her go, move on with his life. Face reality. She was gone, and she wouldn't be coming back.

But he missed touching her. He missed her in his bed, sleeping beside him and seeing her with his children. He missed feeling her laughter against his mouth when he kissed her in the middle of a sentence.

Seeing Kate in the stands yesterday, watching him, had been like a sucker punch to his self-righteous anger. Had he expected her to stay away? Yes. Honestly, he hadn't been sure she gave a damn or even if she was still in town. But she'd come. And the anger he wanted to hold onto now just felt like a burden he wanted to shed. But he had no idea what to do with it.

Looking back, he searched his memory for the moments between them when he could have sworn she was falling in love with him. If she'd been lying about her feelings, wouldn't he have seen it? Was he that blind in love with her that he couldn't even tell if she was playing him?

But no. She was nothing like Melissa. He'd bet his life on it. What she'd done, she'd done out of fear. Fear that could trace its roots directly back to him, dumping her for Melissa. At least that was honest. Unlike what Melissa had done with that information.

Her excuses about expiration dates for men and not being able to do relationships were bullshit. The woman had deep, powerful relationships everywhere she went, from the kids at her school, to her family, to his own children. So, it was, apparently, with him she couldn't have a relationship. A truth that stung deeper than the lie.

A car he didn't recognize pulled into his driveway. A Mercedes SL convertible with the top down. There weren't too many of *those* around here. The driver wore sunglasses and a baseball cap, but as he pulled closer, Finn recognized him. Like a warning shot over the bow of a ship, adrenaline pumped through him.

Mark Erlewine stepped out of his car, holding a manila envelope and wearing a smile on his face.

The hell—?

He got to his feet and met Mark at the bottom of the porch stairs. "Mark. What a surprise. What are you doing all the way down here? The hearing's tomorrow."

"I know," Mark said, shaking Finn's hand. "That's why I'm here. I drove down to give you the news in person. I didn't want to tell you over the phone."

He felt the sudden, pounding need to sit down. Had the judge already ruled? Had he by-passed the hearing altogether when he'd learned about what they'd done? He beckoned Mark up the steps and offered him one of the two paint-shedding Adirondack chairs sitting there.

"It's good news," Mark preempted, before Finn could get a word in.

His insides took a tumble. "It is?"

Mark handed the envelope to him. Inside was a thin file,

labeled, Melissa Jamison. "A copy of this file was turned over to Mrs. Jamison's attorneys yesterday and this one came to me. Within an hour of receipt of that file, I got a phone call from her attorneys, officially cancelling the hearing. Mrs. Jamison has withdrawn her claim."

"She *what*?" He blinked down at the still closed file.

"It's over, Finn. She's dropped out."

His hand shook as he opened the file. Inside was a thorough investigation of his ex-wife, her drug history, her alcoholism, her battle for recovery and her several failures. Then, her marriage to Peter Jamison, a wealthy businessman, who traded international commodities and ran several businesses. One of them in Hong Kong. There was also a complete financial breakdown of his wealth, along with a copy of a pre-marital agreement with Melissa and contingencies regarding children.

"The most interesting, and certainly the most damaging item, is in a sleeve of its own," Mark said, pointing to a letter and a copy of a receipt of money.

Finn read it, stunned, and looked up at Mark. "She enrolled them in a boarding school? In Hong Kong? A *boarding* school? She didn't even want to *keep* them?"

"Boom!" Mark said, grinning. "The boarding school was all very private and hush-hush. She hadn't disclosed any of this to either her attorneys or to the judge. Or, apparently, her husband. When her attorneys found out what our side had discovered, they surely advised her that if there's one thing Judge Corillo likes less than mothers not raising their own children, its mothers who want nothing to do with their children once they have them."

Anger, swift and sharp, rose in him at what she'd tried to do. At how easily she could have shattered both him and their children without giving a damn thought to the consequences. "Why?" he asked. "Why would she do it?"

"I was not privy to the conversation between Mr. and Mrs. Jamison, but I think it's fair to assume this whole thing wasn't about the children at all. More likely, from what I saw in the file, she had some plan to overcome her pre-marital agreement. She drew her check for the boarding school tuition from a private account, separate from their mutual account. Let's just say that the opposing attorney 'indicated' to me that her husband had been 'unhappy and unknowledgeable' about certain contents of the file. Since their case was dropped so quickly, I can only assume he was the one to shut the hearing down. His attorneys, his checkbook."

Finn leaned his head back on the back of the chair. "So…it's really over?"

"Yes. They have already filed a motion to dismiss. I have a copy. If she ever tries to file again, her intentions in this case will likely shut her down. But I don't think she will."

"I…I don't know how to thank you, Mark. I don't know how you managed to dig all this up, but—"

Mark held out a hand and Finn shook it, wanting to hug the man. Wanting to go and wake up the twins and wrap his arms around them. He couldn't believe this was real.

"I wish I could take credit," Mark was saying, "but this wasn't me. A man named Trey Reyes delivered these files to me in person yesterday. Now, the legal world in Montana is a rather small one. I've heard of this guy. He an out-of towner with quite a reputation for demolishing seemingly good cases. I've also heard he does a lot of work for your wife's father."

Dumbfounded, he blinked at Mark. "You mean...Kate's father? But...I just met him the other night. He doesn't even know about—" He stuttered to a stop. "Wait, you mean *Kate hired him...?*"

Mark shrugged. "Reyes didn't reveal that. But there are only two of you in this little pretend, secret marriage and I think we can safely assume that it wasn't you."

"But she never..." he started, but then he laughed, shoving two hands through his hair. *Of course* she never told him. Why would this secret be any different?

Because she just saved your ass. That's why. He could only guess why she'd kept this from him. The potential for failure, she didn't want to get his hopes up. Suddenly, all of her convoluted reasoning of the other night began to make some crazy kind of sense to him. Not that he was all right with her keeping secrets from him, but...

Before he had time to wrap his head around this new revelation, from down the road came a large truck that pulled into his driveway beside Mark's Mercedes. He stood slowly. Surely this day could not get any stranger.

The truck carried ladders and piles of long strips of corrugated metal that looked suspiciously like barn roofing material and various and sundry other building materials.

"Can I help you?" he asked the small, Hispanic man climbing out of his truck.

"No, *señor*," the man replied with a big smile. "It is I who will help you." He reached a hand out to Finn to shake. "I am José Delgado, *señor*. I am here to fix your barn roof."

What? "But I didn't…I can't—there must be some misunderstanding."

"No, no, *señor*. Miss Canaday say today is your *cumpleaños*. Your birthday, no? Is my pleasure to fix. I already come out to look. You don't need a new roof. Just repair. My son and me, we do it today. No charge." He handed him a business card that said he was a licensed and bonded roofer.

No charge? He blinked up at the man. "*What?*"

"*Sí, señor.* Miss Canaday, she taught my younger boy last year to read. He was not even her student. He was in the *fifth* grade. She stayed after school every day to help him when they were all ready to give up. I owe her."

Relationships, Finn thought.

Delgado patted a fist against his chest. "I think and I think, what I can do to pay her back? And when she come to me for this, then…."

"When *did* she come to you?"

He shrugged. "A few weeks ago. She offered me money, but I say *no*. And that is that. We will start now, okay? *Feliz Cumpleaños, señor.* Happy birthday."

Speechless, he could only grab the man's hand again in thanks and watch as the two got back into the truck to drive closer to the barn.

Mark moved beside him. "Things are looking up, eh?" He gestured at Finn's half-casted hand as he slid off his coat jacket. "You know, it's been awhile since I got my hands dirty. And I've got two of 'em and I drove all the way here, it'd be a shame to waste the trip."

"You're kidding me, now, right?"

He made a face. "What? You think we lawyers don't know how to wield a hammer? I'm from Montana, man. Once a country boy, always a country boy. Just so happens I brought a change of clothes."

Still reeling, he showed Mark where to change after retrieving his things from the car. When he was alone again, he took out his cell and dialed Kate. Her voicemail picked up. "Kate?" he said after a long pause. "Please call me. Okay?"

A hundred questions rolled through his mind and he had the answers to none. Kate was nothing if not complicated. Life with a woman like her would never be boring. That was for sure. But she was like the eight second ride that eluded him. The prize he could hold, but could never keep. She'd fake-married him, single-handedly saved his kids from disaster, called in favors for him and then walked away. Who *did* that? And still, he'd blamed her for keeping her secrets and not believing in him.

And she'd let that pass.

Damn the woman!

The sound of more cars pulling into his driveway brought him back to the screen door where he saw what looked like Kate's family stopping at the end of his drive. A cold sweat broke out as he imagined what they'd come to say to the man who'd just broken Kate's heart. How could he explain what had happened between them? And should he? He wasn't even sure he could explain the situation to himself.

He pushed open the screen door as Olivia and Eve came up the porch steps, carrying...brownies?

He opened the door for them and they smiled. "Hi, Finn! We heard it's your birthday and that there are a few things that need doing around here. So we came to help."

"You... Wait. W*hat*?" he stammered.

Olivia set the pan of brownies down on the kitchen table. "Jake couldn't make it. He's flying today, but the rest of us brought tools."

Indeed, there was a box of tools coming up the porch steps in Reed Canaday's arms.

"Happy Birthday," Eve said, brightly.

"Thanks. But did...Kate—?"

"Put us up to this?" Olivia asked. "Who else? And—" she made a sympathetic face—"even though she's not here, we figured we all took the day off anyway. We might as well show up." Reed, Jaycee and his foreman, Ken, hovered at the front door.

"Wow, that really wasn't—Listen, I don't know how to say this, but…Kate and I…we aren't…"

Cutter and Caylee tumbled into the room, still blurry from sleep, but eyes wide at the sight of a roomful of people. "Brownies!" Cutter exclaimed, making a beeline for the chocolate treats.

"See?" Caylee said softly to Finn, a smile creeping to her mouth.

He didn't want to break her heart and tell her Kate hadn't come with the rest of them. The brownies were just a coincidence. That this was all some giant misunderstanding that a simple explanation would clear up and then they would go. But his daughter wandered to the window, pressing her nose against the glass.

"What's that, Daddy?"

In the distance an unfamiliar sound joined the rhythmic clatter of hammering from the barn. A whap-whap-whap sound. What *was* that?

"*Incoming*," Olivia announced.

In fact, a helicopter was heading their way, sweeping down the slope of foothills that rose just beyond his ranch. What the hell? And then he remembered. Jake flew helicopters. But… there was…*music* coming from the helicopter through some kind of a speaker. And as the chopper drew closer he recognized the song.

Richie Havens was singing "*Follow*."

"Hmm. Maybe you should go see," Eve suggested, but he was already halfway out the door by the time she finished her sentence.

Jaycee and Reed stepped back from the door with knowing looks. "We'll watch the kids."

The chopper landed in his pasture, purring and powering down as the song poured out from the speaker. He couldn't see inside the chopper, except for the pilot who was turned his way, watching him come. He lifted his dark glasses with a thumbs up gesture. *Jake.*

"*Let your hands tie a knot across the table, come, touch the things you cannot feel,*" Richie sang.

Still two hundred feet from the helicopter the door slid open to reveal Kate, standing inside, watching him. She jumped down from the doorway and started toward him and the wind from the still-spinning blades whipped her red hair in a froth around her face. She grabbed her mane and gathered the mess in one hand as she walked his way.

"*Then don't mind me 'cos I ain't nothin' but a dream. And you can follow.*"

Finn began to run.

KATE COLLIDED WITH him halfway there and wrapped her arms around him. The comfort of his solidness was a balm, slowing her racing heart and easing her fear. Burying her face against his shoulder, she said, "Oh, thank God you didn't run the other way."

Blinking, he pulled her back by the shoulders, his rough gaze meeting hers. "I *never* wanted to run, Kate."

"No, that was me. But this wouldn't have been much of a grand gesture if you had."

He glanced at the helicopter, then back at the house where her family waited. "Is that what this is? All of this?"

"Oh, well, no, that? They're here because you need help and that's what family does. You are still technically related. The grand gesture part, aside from Jake's helicopter, is *this*."

She touched his face with both hands, then slid them down to his chest. "I realized that I've been running for a long, long time. I ran, even before you could…to Florence. Away from what we had. You were right about that. I didn't even fight for you when you married Melissa. Because I was scared. And hurt and angry. And none of those things kept me warm the next six years. Or kept me from making a fool of myself with men who didn't give a damn about me and who couldn't have been more wrong for me.

"And none of those things that made me run mattered at all when I saw you on that playground that day when Cutter fell. Because I'd never stopped loving you. Never. I've loved you for so long, I was just scared—and I'm still scared—to think that things might actually be good for us only to have them ripped away again. But that's the coward in me—"

"Shhh," he whispered against her forehead. "I don't

know anyone braver than you."

She blew out a laugh. "No. Coward's the right word. I was scared. And wrong. And *scared*. I messed up. But I hope it's not too late. Because this is me, fighting for you. No more lies or secrets. This is my grand gesture, Finn, so there'll be no mistake this time. So, if you can't forgive me, I'll be able to say I gave us my best shot. I fought for you. I didn't walk away without telling you what was in my heart. That I love you."

"You do?"

She nodded tearily. "So much."

Finn glanced off into the fields surrounding his house as if he might find some answers there.

"You said, forgive you?" he whispered, looking back at her with a stroke of his knuckles against her cheek. "I'm grateful. What you did? The kids? They're going to stay with me now. And that was all you."

Grateful? Is that all he was? She braced herself for failure. "Technically, that was Trey Reyes. He's kind of a…dark and twisty miracle work—"

He stopped her words with his mouth. Kissed her so lightly at first, she wasn't sure if he was simply tasting her, or—

"We'll talk about him later."

Or, that would work, too…

Then he dropped his mouth fully on hers and tucked his hand against the back of her head, pulling her even closer.

This time, his kiss felt like coming home, like relief, and the sweetest gift she'd ever been given. Their tongues danced together in a hungry slide that sent a rush of hope through her. Hope and a spark of heat that always settled in her belly when he was near.

Jake had turned off the music and shut down the chopper and she could hear, back at the house, her crazy family erupting into cheers at the sight of them kissing. She imagined they'd all been holding their collective breaths. Right along with her.

He broke the kiss after a long moment and rested his forehead against hers. "Just so we're clear, and before we go run that gauntlet back at our house, I love you, too. And I choose you, Kate. I choose *you*. God knows, I've made my share of mistakes, but all of them led us right here, which makes me lucky as hell for the second chance.

"This thing that just happened between us, that wasn't easy or…in any way close to the way I'd hoped to win you back. But I'll take you any way I can get you. And this time, I'm not letting you go. I want to marry you again, for real, without the lies and the courthouse. With your family all around us and our children beside us. I love you with everything I have…which… may not be a lot right now, but I promise you, I'll make our lives good."

She smiled as tears leaked out of her eyes, and stood on her tiptoes to press a kiss against his mouth. "We'll do that together. You and me and the kids. All of us. I love them more than I can say. And yes. Yes, I'll marry you again. And again. As many times as you want. Because this is where I belong. This is where I want to stay. Right here with you."

His grin widened and he wrapped his arm around her shoulder. "Thank God." Together they headed back toward the house that would be theirs and the family that would surround them with love.

"By the way," she murmured, with her head resting against his shoulder as they walked. "Happy Birthday. Jake's gonna give you a ride in his helicopter."

"He *is*?" He cast a backward look as Jake climbed out of the helicopter to follow them back to the house.

"Uh-huh. And, while I can't top that, I did make you brownies."

"Don't underestimate yourself," he said, that wicked grin of his returning. "And, about the brownies? Caylee never doubted you."

She sighed. "Ahhh. Girl power. And what about you?"

He smiled down at her. "Hey, I'm just a man, navigating the waters of a complicated and amazing woman. Eventually, I came to my senses."

Hugging his arm, she whispered, "Thank God. But just so you know, I'll always be complicated. Apparently, it comes with the territory."

"And I'll always love that about you. That," he added, "and your brownies."

"I can work with that." Threading her fingers through

his, they walked side by side toward the children who were already scampering across the field toward them.

It was the first of many such days together, she hoped; all of them, a family. And for a girl who wasn't born yesterday, Kate Canaday-Scott knew she'd finally been *had*, in the best of all possible ways.

The End

You'll love the next book in the Barbara Ankrum's bestselling series….

The Canadays of Montana

The Canaday clan is like so many modern families today: blended, flawed and full of love for each other. The series follows the Canaday sisters—Olivia, Kate and Eve—strong yet vulnerable women who have careers and challenges that most of us face as they search for balance in their lives.

Book 1: *A Cowboy to Remember*

Book 2: *Choose Me, Cowboy*

Book 3: *The Christmas Wish*

Book 4: *A Cowboy to Keep*

Available now at your favorite online retailer!

About the Author

Barbara Ankrum has a thing for the West and has written both historical and contemporary romances, all set in that magical place. Twice nominated for RWA's RITA Award, her bestselling books are emotional, sexy rides with a touch of humor. Barbara's married and raised two children in Southern California, which, in her mind, makes her a native Westerner.

Thank you for reading

Choose Me, Cowboy

If you enjoyed this book, you can find more from all our great authors at TulePublishing.com, or from your favorite online retailer.

TULE
PUBLISHING

Made in the USA
Coppell, TX
02 May 2022

77312552R10148